A BACK ROOM IN SOMERS TOWN

A BACK ROOM
IN SOMERS TOWN

John Malcolm

All the characters and events portrayed in this work are fictitious.

A BACK ROOM IN SOMERS TOWN

A Felony & Mayhem mystery

PRINTING HISTORY
First UK edition (Collins Crime Club): 1984
First U.S. edition (Charles Scribner's Sons): 1985
Felony & Mayhem edition: 2007

ISBN-10: 1-933397-79-9
ISBN-13: 978-1-933397-79-5

Manufactured in the United States of America

The icon above says you're holding a copy of a book in the Felony & Mayhem "Traditional" category. We think of these books as classy cozies, with little gunplay or gore but often a fair amount of humor and, usually, an intrepid amateur sleuth. If you enjoy this book, you may well like other "Traditional" titles from Felony & Mayhem Press, including:

For more about these books, and other Felony & Mayhem titles, or to place an order, please visit our website at:

www.FelonyAndMayhem.com

or contact us at:

Felony and Mayhem Press
156 Waverly Place
New York, NY 10014

A BACK ROOM IN SOMERS TOWN

1

Q<small>UITE OFTEN, WHEN THE RAIN</small> comes slanting out of the grey London sky, drenching the trees in Hyde Park outside my office window, I think of a back room, another back room, in São Paulo, where the slatted bright stripes of sunlight fell across the rumpled bedclothes and warm skin, like a painting by Bernard Dunstan. They are in a well-established tradition, those voluptuous nudes in early morning bedrooms, and Dunstan paints them well, in a series of light splashes of colour. The effect is cheerful and desirable, without the gloom of a Mornington Crescent interior darkened by the dressing mirror in a grimy window that faces north-east.

Instead of the electric light of a winter's morning I can still see the bright white tiger-stripes across her body, sliding over her as she turned slowly, and I can remember closing the angle of the venetian blind to shut off the hot sun and keep the cool shade of morning. There is no passion like Latin passion. Outside hot climates, the body's desires have to be carefully fuelled and more deliberately stoked than they need be in places where the skin is warm without clothes or central heating.

There is no regret in these memories. When it is remarked that I have a quiet smile on my face despite the rain, it is because the memory is a warm one, despite the remembered dangers and deaths that go with it. It is not a wishful desire for retrogression, or for a going back. I do believe, though, that a person can lead different lives and pick up each thread quite easily again after it has fallen for a while. In this case I do not remember all the words very well; just the opening phrase that snapped me to attention, when it all started, in Motcomb Street.

'All right, Mr Clever Dick,' Willie Morton said, leaning back against his pedestal desk and perching his plump arse on the polished top. 'Tell me about those two paintings. You're the expert. What d'you reckon?'

I had to smile at him. Willie, like many in the fine art trade, adopted an aggressive attitude towards new entrants from whom he hoped to extract money. It would be no good to reiterate, as I had done on several occasions before, that I didn't hold myself up to be a real art expert. He already knew that. But because, in a sense, he reluctantly had to think of me as a client, someone who held part of his life in thrall, the aggression was there. So, to humour him, I played his little game and looked at the two paintings.

Outside his brightly stuccoed gallery façade, Motcomb Street made muted sounds. Willie's was close to Sotheby's Belgravia, almost opposite Motcomb's restaurant and deep in the heart of that creamily classical area known as Belgravia. Other galleries, small but expensive, mingled with antique shops, wine merchants and brasseries. It seemed unlikely that, close by, there were pubs and mews where, in the old days, you could have seen Christine Keeler and gang members of the Great Train Robbers supping their ale. Willie, along with most of his profession, affected the clothes associated with finance rather than fine art; a dark pinstriped suit, crisp white collar, Church's black brogues. Only his tie, bright scarlet, and red carnation buttonhole provided that just too flashy a finish to mark him as a true City man. Willie never looked out of place along in the Saracen's Head at the corner of Kinnerton Street where other dealers drank their lunch. In that part of Belgravia, embassies, Arabs, politicians, horse thieves and hooray henries all mingled quite comfortably.

The two paintings stood side by side on an easel. They were not large. The one on the left was about fifteen inches wide by perhaps eighteen high, framed in a dusty moulding of the old, gessoed type. The immediate impression was of dark, almost sepia, heavily-accented impressionist application of paint. It depicted a depressing London bedroom of pre-1914 vintage, dark, with an iron-grated fireplace. Light from one window slanted across the room, creating heavy shadows. On the iron bedstead, under the window so that the flesh, the coarse fat flesh, was lividly highlighted, lay a very nude woman, aged about forty. Her arm was crooked under her head on the pillow, raising her bloated face and dark hair, but she looked upwards at the ceiling, not seeing her own heavy lolling breasts, so prominently displayed. Her feet were towards the viewer, but one leg was drawn up, knee cocked outwards, so that the dark pubic vee was startlingly thrust at the vision. It was a stark, shocking display, not for the squeamish. She could not have been more prominently presented except, perhaps, if she had been painted by Lucien Freud half a century later. Her gross sexuality glared at me.

Seated close by the bed, on a stiff wooden chair, in an attitude of semi-despair, was a man, also fat and coarse, moustached, middle-aged. He was wearing one of those thick English suits of the Edwardian period, in a dark material but with the jacket removed, so that his waistcoated body had two livid white-shirted arms to it. He sat hunched forward, head in hands, elbows on knees, looking down at the floor and his brown-booted feet. There was an atmosphere of disgust about the scene; it was not clear if he had already spent his passion, having merely removed his jacket before mounting that naked flesh, so that buttons, watch-chain and coarse serge material would have printed themselves, rasping, on the pressed, porcine surfaces, or whether he was re-dressing after a more comprehensive disrobement. Another alternative that struck me was whether he had not yet started, and, having removed his jacket, was gloomily contemplating the sad, lustless, mechanical copulation to come.

I whistled softly.

'Sickert,' I said. 'The Camden Town Murders. Around nineteen-nine? He did several of them. Caused quite a stir. Lot of distaste for Sickert afterwards. But he's the key figure for modern British painting.'

'Bravo,' drawled Willie, lighting himself a cigarette

and narrowing his eyes into the smoke. 'But not too difficult. Now what about the other one?'

The right-hand painting was about the same size. The tones were similar, but lighter. The technique was similar too, but not as heavily applied. There was less sepia, more green, more light, altogether a lighter touch, but still an interior, impressionistic. A bedroom again, pre-1914, with a girl sitting on the bed. This time she was young and fully clothed. She wore a straw boater with a dark band round it, a blouse and a dark pleated peasant skirt with a white apron. She was a simple, clear-skinned girl of perhaps eighteen or nineteen. Her shawl had come off her shoulders and lay around her in a pool as she sat on the edge of the bed, looking, half-sideways, at the floor as though coming to a decision. Standing up, leaning casually against a heavy chest of drawers with a dressing mirror on it, was a young man with a cigarette drooping from the corner of his mouth. He, too, had no jacket on, and his waistcoated, slender figure was in shirtsleeves. There was an attitude of arrogance in the set of his centre-parted head, the cigarette, the way he looked down at the girl on the bed. Behind him was a washstand, and an enamel water jug stood on the floor below it, as though it had just been used.

'Don't tell me,' I said. 'It's called "Drop 'em" or "Get your knickers off".'

'Now come on, Tim. Who painted it? And what do you think of it?'

It was a disturbing picture. Set alongside the Sickert, it was even more so. Something about the imminent exploitation or tragedy, the loss of innocence implied in the scene, was deeply saddening. The young man was so clearly from another world to that of the girl; wealthier, more confident, arrogant. He was going to get what he wanted; perhaps had already had it; and he obviously looked down on her. It provided a sort of link and contrast simultaneously to the Camden Town Sickert. Perhaps the girl would become like the blowsy whore in the other scene; perhaps the slim young man would fail, coarsen, buy whores instead of seducing willing girls. Perhaps he was already corrupting the girl with money. The realism of the two scenes was hard to take: it was too near the bone; there was an inevitability about the two pictures that brought to mind all one's crassest indulgences.

'Well?' Willie jerked my thoughts back.

'Oh, I'd say it's by a follower of Sickert. School of Sickert. One of his ladies, perhaps. Sylvia Gosse—yes, could be by Sylvia Gosse, very easily?'

'No.'

'Oh. Well, try again, then, another of his ladies like say, Wendela Boreel or, what was the one he married third and last, Therese Lessore, yes, that's it, Therese Lessore?'

'No, but not a bad guess. Mary Godwin.'

'Who?'

'Mary Godwin. She's in the book, went to Sickert's School, the one he ran with Sylvia Gosse. Exhibited quite a bit, New English Art Club, Leicester Gallery, all the right places. This isn't called "Knickers" or "Drop 'em," it's called "The Back Room." There's a label on the back. What do you think they are worth, though?'

'Come on, Willie. You know better than that. Asking me to lead with my chin.'

He grinned. I hoped he really didn't think I was that green. The seller is the one who puts the price down first, not the buyer. It's obvious. But because I represented something entirely different, something the trade were not really used to, they'd try anything once. Not that I thought of Willie in the same way as I did the rest of the trade. Perhaps that was my weakness: buying and selling is all about relationships. Willie was working well.

He pulled on his cigarette again and cocked his head at me, still smiling. There was something very confident about him, unusually so, like a man who's just had his luck turn. I felt that he was playing with me.

'We're men of the world, you and me,' he said. 'Let's not pretend. I'm a dealer in paintings; you're an investment man, loaded with facts and figures and charts and graphs, all stacked up in that Park Lane office where Jeremy White's little caper goes on.'

An element of mockery had crept into his voice. He might have seen a stiffening of my features or he might not, but his tone dropped the mockery as he went on, more seriously.

'We both follow the form book, in other words. You, maybe more statistically; me more from gut reaction.'

'Bugger gut reaction, Willie. You're like any horse-racing gambler and placeman combined. You know who the punters are for a given type of painting and how much they'll pay. I'm a possible punter and we both know it, but remember I have to think longer term than you.'

'All right, all right. Don't lose your wool. Come on now, Tim, without looking at your files and records and all those catalogues, auction price lists, results and all the rest; be a dealer for a change and chance your arm. How much?'

I smiled at him. 'I'm not a dealer and my whole essence is based on checking records, just as yours is. Look at all those same reference books and auction catalogues on the shelves behind you. What are you asking me? What I could buy the paintings for at auction, say one of our famous houses like Christerby's of London, Paris and New York fame? Or what I have to pay a smart Motcomb Street gallery with a one hundred per cent mark-up for them?'

He flushed slightly. Dealers and auctioneers live together in a somewhat incestuous relationship, sometimes loving, sometimes hating each other. It is not always cheapest to buy at auction, or vice-versa.

'You're the investment man. Stop flannelling. You're out on the market. What are you prepared to pay for a really good Sickert?'

'About fifteen thousand.'

He pulled a face. 'The last one sold in Bond Street was twenty-five, for God's sake.'

'That was a Venetian scene. Or a Dieppe. Not a Camden Town job. Is this one in any of the books, like Wendy Baron, by the way?'

He avoided the question. I could tell that his mind had moved on. Something I had said had reassured him. Perhaps by starting at fifteen thousand, I had established for him that twenty might be possible. Willie had been having a tough time for a while: this might be a break.

'What about the other one? The Mary Godwin?'

I shrugged. 'About five hundred, I would think, at the most. You might get the Fine Art Society to bid it up a bit. Or even Michael Parkin, down the road. Apart from you, that is.'

He made a mocking wince. The Fine Art Society is in Bond Street but Parkin is just down Motcomb Street and a specialist on Sickert's ladies. Willie looked upon him as the opposition.

'It all depends,' I said heavily, leaning forward to deliver the crunch question, 'on the provenance. What provenance is there? Where are they from? What books are they recorded in?'

He looked me straight in the eye.

'They're not recorded,' he said, but without any concern in his voice at all for what should have been a diminution of the paintings' credibility. Indeed, he was almost like a man about to produce a trump card.

'Why not?'

'You and your bloody books and records! They are not recorded, young feller, because these two paintings are part of a complete collection of British paintings of the period nineteen hundred to nineteen-fourteen which has an impeccable provenance, but which has only just come on to the market—I should say into my hands—for disposal.'

'Impeccable provenance? Where from? And, with all due respect to you, Willie, why isn't the collection being sold by Christerby's? That's the logical thing for any big collector who wants to attract all the right buyers, because of the publicity they'll guarantee.'

He put a finger to the side of his nose. 'That's just it. Publicity. The client doesn't want any.'

'Eh?'

'You see, young Tim, there are more things in

heaven and earth than you wot of, or whatever it is. The Client lives abroad. Abroad means wogs, dagoes and chinamen. Dutchmen and snivelling blackamoors. People who have funny rules about moving money about. Unlike our own dear queen, Maggie, bless 'er. My client tries to move an art collection worth three hundred thousand nicker or upwards of that to London to sell with attendant publicity and what will his local tax man say, eh? And the VAT. They'll not only clobber him from the Inland Revenue or whatever they have, but there'll also be all hell to pay for illegally contravening exchange control, export of valuable works of art essential to the National Heritage, obstructing a police officer in the course of his duty and bringing down the foundations of the National Exchequer. My client wants these paintings quietly disposed of at a decent market value by a good reputable dealer and no aggravation. Follow me?'

He leaned across and tapped me on the chest. 'You play your cards right, Timmy boy, and I'll see that that investment fund of yours that you and Jeremy are so keen on will get some really beezer stuff at really right prices.'

I looked back at the paintings. Intense interiors, heavy with encrusted wallpaper, coal fires and enamel jugs. The barren boredom of men or women hooked into relationships that seemed interminable, unbreakable, bound by a legal system that must have been stifling and cruel. I am a sucker for the passions of these interiors; a home-loving boy, my mother used to say. Before I started playing rugby, that was.

I walked to the door. 'All right, Willie,' I said, 'let me have the details of the rest of the collection and the provenance and I'll come and see them. You know me. I'm not committing myself or the fund, but it is up our street. You and your client must know one thing, though. There aren't many people you can go to who have the clout to buy the lot. The whole collection.'

Willie grinned. 'Actually, the Godwin's not for sale, for sentimental reasons,' he said. 'But it's the least of the bunch. We could sell such important paintings, like those I'm told are in the collection, one at a time, piece-meal.'

'And take a long time. Clients like yours usually want a nice quick lump sum, not bits and pieces over a period.'

He shook his head doubtfully. 'I don't think so. I don't really know, though. The client's man is coming to tell me about the rest of it, later. Now I know you're interested I'll get you full details, don't worry.'

'All right. But no promises.'

He nodded, relaxed. Once he had one interested party in his pocket he'd probably tour around, picking up a second, a third. Perhaps. I wasn't sure if Willie was a Dutch auction type, but he was certainly capable of it.

I closed the gallery door and stood out in Motcomb Street. They were loading crates of claret at the wine merchant's, and the December sun shone weakly on the colonnaded Pantechnicon façade. There was nothing in Motcomb Street to bring darkness into the mind, like murderous intent and lustful coupling in borrowed rooms. Except the paintings, of course.

2

Jeremy White's 'little caper' in Mayfair was an insurance broking office specializing in personal investment advice for those who have the problem of coping with too much money. You would have thought, if you had been used to factories, offices, monthly pay cheques and despondent bank managers, like me, that it wouldn't last long. Not a bit of it: it was boom time for insurance investment bonds, which the current Chancellor of the Exchequer had no plans to ruin for a while. Thousands were being helped, by an allowance in the law benefiting profitable insurance schemes, and by willing insurance companies, to pour their money into bonds.

There were all sorts of bonds. Bonds based on investing in property, land, industry, gold, shekels, oil, the Far East, combinations of the lot and anything else that sharp-lapelled pinstriped City wonders could think of, sometimes in combination with transatlantic, or transcontinental, mohair-suited men. What really staggered me was the amount of money that was forthcoming, in great lumps, from people who filled in response advertisements in newspapers, or who just walked in off the street. Then there were lawyers, with clients needing advice on investment, and accountants, and landowners, and retired people and successful executives, some of them selling insurance bonds...

The great advantage that Jeremy White had was that, brought up with money, he knew how to talk to people with money; people with big money. How they felt and worried and didn't worry; what needled them and what they wanted to conserve. The rumour that the name White was anglicized from Weiss was never overtly mentioned. He was an unusually generous employer, inefficient, rewarding his key men lavishly. The office in Park Lane was housed in one of the double-fronted elegantly-curved mansions overlooking the Park, that his type of family would have used as their town house until the First World War. It had been much subdivided inside for office use, but the moulded ceilings and friezes, the height of rooms and the long French windows with their leafy outlook still gave a feeling of comfortable superiority.

Jeremy was a tall, blond, young-looking man, slightly bulky, but in no way yet fat. He was now in his early forties, patrician but friendly, confident but never aggressive. Like many well-connected younger men with City foundations, his mind had always been occupied with the creation and preservation of personal wealth. It came quite naturally to turn a personal preoccupation into a successful business despite the intense disapproval of the family bank, who regarded bond broking as a fly-by-night affair.

Jeremy came from the White family of merchant wankers, as he called them. His relationship, as a younger man of a cadet branch, with the Bank's directors, who included his uncle, the chairman, and his father as a director, was problematical. White's were stuffy. They had been founded a long time ago by a trading ancestor who would have regarded banking as a supine activity for a man of energy.

'Bird shit, wasn't it?' I once asked Jeremy.

He gaped at me, startled.

'Guano,' I explained. 'From Peru. Imported as fertilizer in the nineteenth-century. Got South American connections like me, haven't you?'

He burst into a roar of high-pitched Etonian laughter. 'No, no,' he hollered. 'Not us. That's Antony Gibbs you're thinking of. Built a mansion with it, down Somerset way. Called Tyntesfield. High Church Gothic, forgot the guano. Frightfully stuffy ever since, just like our lot. No, we were timber. Rosewood, mahogany. From Brazil. All that Regency and early Victorian furniture. You should know. Solid and veneers. Still a frightfully good business, actually, or was. Not so much Brazil now, though, more Far East. The British have, shall we say, receded somewhat in South America. We still have a good timber business in Brazil but it's mostly local. Frightfully difficult to get one's money out, even as exporters. There's a branch of the family still out there, been there donkey's years. My cousin, at Eton before me. Very pukka, trying to be more English than the English. It's often the way. His grandfather was at the Slade. Never exhibited. Odd story.'

He mused for a moment, then changed the subject to some problem with accounts. I wasn't working for him, then. Jeremy's office systems were hopeless and he knew it; they were hopeless because such things bored him intensely. He took the simple expedient of hiring business consultants to sort out the mess, prevent the odd cheques for twenty thousand getting dropped in the coffee or lost in the photocopier, and to recruit a decent accountant. That was what I was doing, until the accountant arrived, recruited from a suitably with-it advertising agency to ensure that there would be some continuity in changing from one con game to another. Jeremy White advertised a lot, sold advice on how to make money work, and took a percentage. It was all the same idea. The new man settled in happily.

I had early on realized that Jeremy and White's Bank had an uneasy relationship. He liked the serious image that association with the bank gave his operation. It reassured the clients. Founded 1780, mansion in the City, part of the financial establishment, that sort of thing. In practice, it ended there. He regarded the Bank as backward, hidebound, unenterprising and half-baked. The fact that he was looked upon by his uncle and father as a young idiot, just out of school, wet behind the ears and financially irresponsible, made the relationship a two-way iceberg. Jeremy was out to prove to the Bank that he could make large sums of money, understand modern financial growth markets, and branch out into new ventures successfully, making him a candidate for future chairmanship. The Bank was waiting for him to fall flat on his face.

After I had been working in Park Lane for a while I found that to talk to Jeremy about what I was doing to his clerical systems was a waste of time. He just paid the fees and watched things get better. Our real level of communication concerned a hobby we both had, even at different levels of financial participation. Jeremy was very interested in interior decor; I was an art and antique collector. He had a very sound knowledge of some of the things people furnish with and the money they were prepared to pay. I had a modestly competent understanding of modem art and an abiding interest in silver, furniture and a few other collectors' passions. Our conversations at what he called his 'canteen'—the Mirabelle in Curzon Street—became proportionately more and more about the auction rooms, galleries and dealers, less and less about coping with a cash flow of forty million pounds.

I owed my interest in art to my ex-wife, Carol. She took me trailing round galleries and antique shops, squeezing through auction rooms and jostling among the canvas-covered stalls in street markets. Her interest was inexhaustible. At first, bored, I would amble round behind her, content to relax after a hard week away, beavering at some company's problems. Then I started to get interested myself, not in the old brown sterile paintings of lousy quality that made up most of what we saw, but in more modern types and objects taking me into earlier twentieth century. Alas, Carol was convinced that only the eighteenth century had any merit in English art and design; the one interest we might have had in common never brought us together. If anything, our divergent tastes drove us further apart.

It was not long before I was sent along to Jeremy White's that we finally tore it all apart. I was working in a rather classy Bond Street perfume manufacturer's offices, feeling like a bull terrier among borzois, and one thing led to another. Divorces are a boring subject: by the time the mess was finally loaded into the dustbin and the lid put on, I was very glad to be given a change. It was unusual for me to have two assignments in a row in London itself. Mostly my specialization was abroad, which hadn't helped Carol and me to get on any better.

At first I regarded Jeremy and his crowd with amusement. My father, whom I had hardly known, left a tradition of hard-working, constructional pioneering in the family which would have been horrified at the perfumes and, now, the wealthy activity I was involved in. Parasitism, he would have called it. After I had got over the immediate amateurism of their office systems I started to change. Anyone can organize office systems. Few can initiate, inspire and enthuse others. I liked Jeremy and, in the absence of Carol, enjoyed our talks on art and antiques. One day, after lunch, when I was a bit off guard, Jeremy asked me back into his office. Geoffrey Price, the new accountant, was in with him. I smelt a set-up.

'Tim,' Jeremy adopted his more public persona to me, the one he put on to give the important clients confidence. 'You know that one of the things I feel we really must do here is to offer all our clients the best possible advice on all aspects of investment.'

'Yes, Jeremy.'

'A complete portfolio, in fact.'

'Indeed.'

'Mostly,' he went on, ignoring my sycophancy, 'people come to us to invest in conventional things—shares, property, unit trusts, all managed properly, of course, in bonds and so on. Growth, income, whatever. But we really have to keep ahead of the others. Longer term and some higher risk business. Like art and antiques, for instance. I saw in the papers the other day that Georgian silver has outperformed the stock market by several times.'

'Dicey thing, silver, Jeremy, I...'

He held up his hand. 'Precisely, Tim. Precisely. That's where I see you coming in. An immediate comment, d'you see. What d'you think? Our specialist in fine art investment, eh? One of us.'

I was flabbergasted. Geoffrey looked at me intently.

'You mean,' I spluttered, 'a sort of adviser? A service to clients?'

Jeremy shook his head. 'We have to take a lead,' he said. 'For some clients, OK, advise them, steer them to the right type of thing, reliable sources. Just think of the commissions. But I was thinking of more than that. We set up a fund. Invest it in really good art treasures. Manage it.'

'For God's sake, Jeremy,' I said. 'You mean you want to set up your own British Rail Pension Fund?'

He hooted with laughter. 'Not as big as that. You know as well as I do that there are one or two art investment funds about. Not very big and I don't know what they've got. Should we advise our clients to invest in them or not? More to the point, wouldn't they be better off if we did it ourselves?'

'Jeremy, I'm not an art specialist. What about authenticity?'

He waved that aside. 'Get a specialist. Pay a fee if necessary, if you're not buying from auction or a reliable dealer with invoices. Always find an extra specialist. No problem. Technicalities, like pipefitting. Management is the skill I value.'

I had forgotten that Jeremy's mind, like that of his family at the Bank, divided people into three categories where employment was concerned. First, themselves. You could never join them, except by birth or equivalent wealth. Sometimes a foreigner might be allowed equal status nominally, a directorship, because he could make them a lot of money. A foreigner, a Jew, even a Scotsman. No one else. It was a question of pronunciation and background.

Then there were Stewards. People to run the estates, manage the Bank, professionals with good education. They would never be offered directorships at the Bank. Subsidiary companies, maybe, the odd industrial or commercial venture, but not at the Bank. They would be given a small stewardship first, a department to manage, one of the farms to run, then, if all went well, bigger responsibilities. To the Whites, the rest of the world were the workers, some skilled, some unskilled. Thatchers and farmhands, builders and plumbers, computer specialists and art experts. Hewers of wood and drawers of water. The people who actually had to do it. To Jeremy's mind all life was like being in the army; you did your basic training, learnt what all the jobs the soldiery had to do were and then you became an officer, usually on a horse. All very simple.

I was being offered an introduction to stewardship.

Geoffrey Price cleared his throat. 'We've been talking about you, Tim,' he said. 'It isn't only the art investment fund. I'm damn sure you would be an asset to us generally. Jeremy and I both admire the work you've done to set things straight. Means I've been able to come in as a new boy and take over an efficient operation.'

And how useful, I thought, to make sure I stay around to see that things stay straight and to give free consultancy advice to you. But Jeremy, nodding, broke in.

'It's not just that, though. You've got ideas, haven't you Tim? I know you have. What to invest in. Haven't you?'

'Well,' I said slowly, 'there are some obvious things. Take furniture, for example. In the 'twenties and 'thirties oak went to astronomic prices, then slumped badly. Lately it's shot through the roof again. Country furniture too. But good quality mahogany has lagged. It must go up. And modern British painting, from 1890 onwards. It'll never be the same as the French Impressionists or anything like that but it's very undervalued. It must go—'

Jeremy was clapping his hands. 'Bravo! You see? You can advise. And I know you can manage. Authenticity is for experts. We can set up a fund. Share the investments. Our members of the fund can have them at home, if properly insured. Think of it. We are insurance brokers. We get the premiums. It's superb.'

'There is an investment risk, though, Jeremy. People can't just move in and out like they can with bonds. I suppose you revalue the stuff every year, like a stocktake, but—.'

'But, but! Risk! Tim, some of our clients and friends are paying ninety-eight per cent tax on their upper unearned income. Ninety-eight per cent! If they risk that money and lose the lot—which they won't—they've only really lost two per cent. No wonder Yankee salesmen are doing fabulous business in speculative oil wells. Come on, will you?'

His face shone at me. I thought of the firm I worked for, solid middle-class townee professionals and engineers, computer specialists and production men. I'd been working at Park Lane for four months, for once a decent predictable everyday life. When this job was finished, I'd be back on the road, one assignment after another, here, there, everywhere. I'd be travelling abroad again. My divorce had been through for only a few weeks. Jeremy's venture, I felt sure, was a bubble. Some socialist Chancellor would burst it, or the money would dry up, or something. I had been brought up to believe that good men made things for a living, like boilers or upper cylinder lubricant. Good men didn't ponce around telling people how to buy bits of canvas with paint stuck on and other illusions.

Jeremy was watching me like a hawk. He struck, genially, happily, his face shining. Jeremy was a boy who loved giving people presents. 'Of course,' he smiled, 'I think you'll find the salary acceptable. Should be, eh, Geoffrey?'

'Yes,' said Geoffrey to cue. 'Say a basic of twenty thousand a year? Then our current profitability bonus— that would, at today's rates, add another two or three."

It was a while ago, you understand. 1979. At that time, as a well-regarded beaver in the firm, I was earning, at full stretch, sixteen thousand a year.

'All right, Mr Clever Dick,' as Willie Morton used to say, 'what would you have done?'

3

I CAUGHT A TAXI from Willie Morton's down to Millbank and along to the Tate Gallery. At the porter's desk I asked for the administrative assistant I wanted and then I went along to the Modern British galleries. It was pretty sparse. I was cricking my neck sideways to look at Sicken's "Ennui"—or, I should say, one of Sickert's Ennuis, the one the Tate has got—when she came up softly behind me.

'It's pretty terrible,' I said, 'when you think of what the taxpayer can't see. No other Sickerts on view, no Camden Town Murder Sickerts to look at, can't find Nicholson's still life of silver, not a Rothenstein anywhere despite his lad being one of the Trustees, Lucien Pissaro's snow scene at Coldharbour Lane lent to the Frogs, and where the hell is Gwen John's self-portrait but half a mile downstairs at the end of a back passage? The anus aristicorum, you might say.'

'How unsuitable,' she replied primly, 'for a Park

Lane smoothie to be talking of paying tax. I thought that was what you never did.'

'Not true.' I corrected. 'A broken-nosed ex-rugger player is not a smoothie. I also pay tax. We try to help our clients to avoid paying it. Or, at least, too much of it.'

'That's why you're corrupting the art world with your City funds is it?'

'Assisting the British art market to achieve its real potential, you mean, don't you?'

She smiled, but there was basic disapproval there, somewhere. The blue eyes looked appraising, not accepting. There was a set to her face and stiffness the way the head, with its soft mid-brown hair, was held. She wore a beige pullover and light brown skirt, somehow emphasizing her slenderness. Stockings and brown shoes; all very traditional, very restrained. She glanced about, as though it was a risk to be seen with me.

'The Tate does have one of Sickert's Camden Town Murder paintings, doesn't it?'

'Yes, we do have one.'

'Why isn't it on view?'

'Are you going to go on complaining about the displays or are you going to take me to lunch? Time is short, as I told you.'

'I'm sorry. I'm sorry it has to be here at the Tate, in your home canteen, so to speak.'

Her eyes widened, and she turned to look at me as we walked.

'I did book a table,' I added hastily, 'in the restaurant.'

'Oh. I thought for a moment you meant the buffet. A poor meek administrative assistant on an ignorant assistant's salary can't afford to eat in the restaurant, you know. Not like financiers.'

'Ignorant assistant is not how I would describe a young lady who's done three years at Oxford followed by two at the Courtauld getting a remarkably proficient qualification in Art History. And I'm not a financier.'

We were walking past the big Lowry in the foyer, the one you pass as you go to the staircase down to the restaurant. I remember thinking how, having loved L. S. Lowry when I was sixteen, I'd come to detest most of his work by the time I was thirty. But that big Lowry at the Tate is superb, all white and red and black like a new sampler.

'How did you know that?'

'You told me. The evening before last when we met. Oxford and the Courtauld.'

'But I didn't tell you what sort of passes I got.'

'No, I had to research that.'

She had no time to ask me any more because we'd arrived at the restaurant. There was a certain amount of fussing to the table and settling in. She refused a drink from the waiter. The Tate Gallery restaurant is really quite good; I turned down a pre-meal drink with regret and peered at the menu.

'What research?'

'Eh?'

'How did you research my degrees?'

'Oh. Not a trade secret. You wouldn't have this job if the grades weren't good, would you? Let's order first, shall we, then we can deal with all that.'

It was getting off to a bad start. I'd met her at a party Geoffrey Price had invited me to, at a gallery a friend of his ran in Hampstead. Her name was Sue, Sue

Westerman. I'd made a joke about Percy F. which she found totally incomprehensible and then I'd felt a fool explaining that Percy F. Westerman was a boys' adventure-story writer of the 'twenties and 'thirties, very popular then, and that I'd got a collected edition of him somewhere.

'I didn't think you were that old,' she'd said and I'd laughed obligingly, along with those around us, while realizing how stupid the joke had been. Since the divorce, something had gone wrong with my relationships with the opposite sex. It was as though I was rusty, out of practice. Not until someone made a remark about the Tate and her job had we started any sort of conversation. She was guarded at first, like anyone discussing their own profession, but warmed up on the subject of Stanley Spencer, whom I don't really understand, not being religious myself. She seemed a bit surprised when I'd asked her to lunch, as though she hadn't expected or approved of such invitations from anyone. She accepted, with the proviso that her lunch-break would have to be short.

I can't really explain what attracted me to her. Perhaps because she didn't look like Carol, my lately divorced, unlamented wife. People say that nothing is ever learned by divorcees and that they continue to remarry the same type of person they were entangled with before. It isn't really true, at least I hope it isn't; there would be a terrible fatalism about being condemned to marry the same sort of woman over and over again.

I suppose I had subconsciously thought that she might become a good expert contact for the Fund. We had bought quite a few interesting paintings, some top quality mahogany and a gaggle of smaller things. As a new venture my job was going quite well. I'd got contacts with the auctioneers, some specialist dealers and a reference library that wasn't bad. At the end of my first year I might about break even and, in the second, I thought I'd make a profit for Jeremy and justify my existence. He was quite unperturbed about that, though.

'Don't worry, Tim,' he said. 'You're doing splendidly. It's marvellous PR. Giving us a wide reputation for investment advice. People at the Bank are furious.'

And he'd gone off, chortling to himself. Of course, I had had quite a bit of publicity, which always flattered Jeremy. I wondered if I was not just another part of his extensive advertising budget.

Building up a list of contacts was a good principle, but I was rather nettled when Sue Westerman, having ordered smoked salmon and a poached trout, said, 'I suppose I shall have to get used to dealers and the like coming to pick my brains, as I get more experienced.'

Damn you, I thought. Damn you, for a smug academic moralizing prig. The relationship between male museum experts, traders and auctioneers is quite relaxed. Each has a clear concept of his territorial position and just where he stands.

'Dealers and the like,' I said, carefully emphasizing the 'like', 'are often too knowledgeable to need to pick the brains of others. Let me make it quite clear, though; we at White's pay for any formal expert opinion we seek.'

I put the emphasis on 'expert'. She flushed. 'Until one meets an expert and talks to him—or her—one has no idea what his or her specialization might be and what he or she is interested in developing. It's only by talking that one finds out what mutual benefit there might be.'

That's it, I thought, that's blown it now. This'll be nothing but a tight, business conversation.

The waiter had chilled the bottle of Sancerre I'd ordered and now he poured it out. She took a sip, then she spoke.

'I don't really approve of making money out of art. I hate the whole business of art dealing and buying purely for investment. I hate the manipulation and the forgeries, the using of artists to make money while keeping them down.'

'Down? Like Hockney, you mean? Or Picasso, while he was alive? And let me tell you—museums pay the biggest money for art, not collectors or investors. Even so, owning expensive paintings is like owning racehorses—a rich man's indulgence. Always has been. So you can't dissociate money from art. It does pay your salary too.'

'I know. I just don't like it, that's all.'

She said it simply, not unsympathetically, in a rather touching way.

I tried to turn the conversation.

'Tell me—do you know if Sickert made any money from art?'

She paused over her smoked salmon and looked at me, interested. 'No, I don't. I don't think so. He was broke when he came back to England from France in nineteen-five. He was very prolific. Lot of etchings. And then all those later paintings based on photographs. But the art school he started with Sylvia Gosse—why do that except to raise money? And the Fitzroy Gallery with Saturday invitees. They were all hard up.'

'He was an evangelist a bit, I think. Wanted to show

everyone what to do. Changed British painting. So Wendy Baron's book might not have all his Camden Town paintings in it?'

'Oh God, no. It's almost impossible to record the entire output of any artist. Lots of paintings disappear for ages and then reappear later. If the artist gets famous. Then they're worth while finding and they come pouring out of the woodwork. But Sickerts keep turning up all the time.'

'That's true. But they have to have a provenance to fetch money.'

'Yes, I suppose they do. I'm afraid I don't know much about the money part. But I like Sickert; actually I did a bit of a special study of him.'

The glimmering of an idea came over me.

'And Mary Godwin? D'you know her work?'

The poached trout arrived. She nodded emphatically.

'Yes, she's nice. She was at the Sicken-Sylvia Gosse school. I like her painting; she's not famous or anything, but good. Why?'

'Would you like to look at a Sickert—one of the Camden Town Murders—and a Mary Godwin for me? Give me an opinion? For a fee, of course?'

She sat up, electrified. This time the flush was one of pleasure. Her eyes sparkled. She actually smiled.

'My first consultation! How super! Yes, of course. How much would you, I mean how much should I, oh, I'm being paid by the Tate, you know, and, it's not the money, but I—'

'Relax. Say fifty pounds? No questions asked.'

'Oh. I suppose you think I've gone back on everything I've said, but, well, I do want to be a specialist and to make a name, not for the money, but to build a reputation. You do see, don't you? No, you don't, you're probably as cynical as hell.'

On one of his rare visits home my father once told me, and he was a genuine cynic, that the way to a woman's heart or worse was money. Either it's money direct, he used to say, which is more honest, or money indirect, like presents or holidays or career influence or power and social position. I was young at the time and deplored his middle-aged disenchantment. Now I drank some Sancerre, smiled at Sue Westerman and reflected how right he probably had been.

'Not at all,' I lied. 'I really do understand. You're just starting and you need to be seen around as an expert. I'm in the same condition. If I can give you a tip—hope I'm not teaching my grandmother to suck eggs—you must try to get round the auction rooms a good deal too.'

Sue nodded. 'I know. I must. But I've been occupied getting started here and everything.'

I ordered coffee. She looked at me, a little more interested.

'Tell me,' she said, 'you're not married, are you?'

I shook my head. 'No. And, in case you're wondering why a presentable man of thirty-five isn't married, there's no ear-ring in my right ear, either. I'm not a poofter, I'm divorced.'

She looked at me directly, not saying she was sorry to hear it or anything like that but somehow nodding slightly as though it was what one would have expected from a man in my situation, a 'Park Lane smoothie' doing his best to disrupt the niceties of picture collecting and availability of things for pure-minded museums. But she did make an attempt at sympathy.

'I didn't think you were—a poofter, I mean. I'm sorry to hear things didn't work out—with your marriage, I mean.'

'Call it life,' I replied. 'It takes two to make a divorce, just like a marriage. The immediate cause of the divorce, though, was that my wife found that I was going to bed with another woman.'

Why did I say it? It was the first time I'd come out with it, just like that.

At that precise moment, with impeccable timing, the interruption occurred. Perhaps just as well. Sue stared at me, lips slightly parted, a look in which disapproval and intense interest combined to produce a quizzical uncertainty. The head waiter, however, bending over the table, stopped any verbal response from her.

'Mr Simpson? I'm sorry to disturb you. There is an urgent phone call for you. The switchboard have put it through to my office. Would you like to take it there?'

I gaped at him, flustered. The only person I'd told that I would be at the Tate was my shared secretary at the office. Excusing myself to Sue and thanking the head waiter, I followed him across the restaurant, considerably irritated. Jeremy employed a strain of secretaries who tended to be county girls or semi-debutantes, very svelte and very smooth. There was a senior one who looked after Jeremy himself and was something of a permanent fixture, but the rest were typical West End nomads, giving up jobs to go to the States or skiing or on some fashionable excuse. There was a high turnover.

The man showed me his phone, in a little office near the kitchen, excused himself and accepted my thanks with a smile. I picked up the phone angrily. It was Jeremy's secretary, the senior one. 'Tim? Hello, sorry to bother you, but I had a call about twenty minutes ago and it's taken me a while to find out where you'd gone. I'm sorry to interrupt your lunch but it did seem rather urgent.'

'That's OK,' I had to say, stifling the irritable comment that had come to mind. 'What is it, Penny?'

'A Mr Morton phoned. Seemed very agitated. I took the call because the other girls were at lunch. He said could you see him as soon as possible. Something very urgent, most urgent, he said, something you and he have been discussing.'

'Really? I've only just left him an hour or so ago. Did he say anything more?'

'Only something about an extraordinary coincidence. And something odd. Then he put the phone down suddenly. I thought I'd better tell you.'

'Yes, of course. Thanks, Penny. Leave it with me now. If he calls back, tell him I'm on my way.'

I put the phone down, musing. It was very strange. Willie Morton's whole existence depended on a calm, confident exterior, a poker-player's control, and the hinted reference to the superb benefits of the painting he was presenting. Urgency and oddness and doubt are anathema to the fine art trade.

I tried calling him, dialling round and round with some impatience. There was no reply.

Muttering to myself, I went back to the table and called for the bill. Sue looked at me expectantly.

I figured that Willie had popped out to the Saracen's Head for a quick glass of lunch.

'Look,' I said to Sue, 'I have to dash and see those paintings again now, probably along with some other interesting ones. It's a private pre-view, you might say, and some of them may not surface for some time. The offer still stands. D'you want to come?'

It wasn't until we were in the taxi heading for Willie's that I reflected that for a girl who'd told me originally that she only had a short time available for lunch there had been little hesitation in joining me. Whatever it was that had been going to demand her attention that afternoon had received very short shrift.

One of the maddening things about life, as it goes on, is how often you find that your father was absolutely right.

4

MOTCOMB STREET WAS QUITE crowded, with parked cars and vans, some of them up on the pavement, straddling the yellow no-parking lines. It's often the way. Quite a lot of the galleries and shops have to have deliveries from the front. The taxi-driver threaded his way to a spot near Willie Morton's and I paid him off.

The front door said 'Closed, back in 15 minutes' and I cursed. The gallery lights were out but I could see through to the other end because, like most of those Motcomb Street galleries, Willie's ran right through the building to the windows at the back, giving on to the pedestrian area and grass below the blocks of flats. Willie had an archway dividing his gallery half way; in the rear half was where his desk and office bits were placed.

I had an idea.

'The paintings are on the easel in the back half,' I said to Sue who was waiting nervously. 'Let's look at them through the back window until Willie comes to open up. He'll come to the back door first, anyway. Always does.'

We went through the passage to the back and along to Willie's back door. I tried the handle.

The door opened.

Inside, on the reverse wall of the central arch there was a still life of flowers by James Bolivar Manson, quite nice really, he was secretary of the Camden Town Group, but a bit pricey, and then two drawings by Augustus John of girls, typical, with nude figures and suggestive poses, pubic parts almost detailed. Typical, as I say, of the old bearded goat of a man he was, always insisted on having it off with his models if he could. With about as much ceremony and expertise as a whisky-soaked orangutan jumping on his females in the jungle. And below the Augustus John drawings, on the floor, sticking out from behind Willie Morton's desk was one of Willie Morton's brogues, made by Church's, with Willie Morton's dark wool sock coming out of it and disappearing behind the big partners' desk with the polished top he'd rested his plump arse on two hours or so before.

Behind the partners' desk lying with his head resting against the wall under the bookshelves was Willie Morton, with his red carnation and his red tie. Only his red tie had expanded over his white shirt, all over his white shirt, and the red tie stain spread down his side from the part where a large paper knife had been stuck in his chest to the side of the tie, into his heart, so that Willie Morton was very dead indeed.

The easel facing the desk was empty.

I stepped across the floor to look at the easel and, as

I did so, Sue Westerman, who had given an involuntary gasp, screamed like the bells of hell all going off at action stations, almost drowning the footfall behind me, but not quite, so that I turned and the bastard missed my head.

He must have been behind the arch when we walked in. When I turned towards the easel he'd stepped out and swung with all his force at my head with a heavy brass pillar paperweight he must have picked up from poor Willie's desk. Thanks to Sue, he missed, but his arm came down on my shoulder with all his force and, off balance, he rammed into me so that we collided and shunted backwards into the bloody easel, which collapsed with us on top of it, splintering wood everywhere.

He wasn't heavy, but I was underneath, an easel peg stuck in my kidney and my shoulder was completely numb. The brass weight had clattered off into a corner. He sprang to his feet and I tried to grab his jacket but it was rough tweed and I missed as he lunged to the corner to get the paperweight. I stuck my foot out and floored him, scrummage style, flat on his face, but he rolled over and lunged again, grabbing the weight as he got back to his feet. Sue got her breath back and screamed again, this time even louder. There was a shout from outside. I rolled back deeper into the gallery and got a leg to the floor, recovering. He whirled, struck obliquely at Sue, missing her, and was gone, through the back door and away as Sue's scream ended. There was another shout from outside and then silence. Sue fainted clean away on to the late Willie Morton's best quality Motcomb Street Wilton carpet.

5

It all took a long time to clear up. The man who'd shouted outside called the police. I managed to prop Sue up to revive her and a really helpful citizen came in from a wine merchant's with some brandy. The intruder had got clean away. We sat about in a state of shock as the gallery filled with people.

The police arrived in dribs and drabs; a patrol car, then two bigger patrol cars, then photographers and an ambulance of some sort and fingerprint men; it seemed to go on forever. We had to go down to a police station and make statements, in great detail. I phoned Jeremy's office to tell him what had happened and he immediately sent a young solicitor from the company's lawyers over. It was the sort of prompt kindness that was instinctive to him.

We went through it all over again. Murder is still not that common an occurrence in London and murder in the pursuit of theft is even less so. The papers, particularly the evening papers, for whom it was timed quite well, made a splash of it; the 'Motcomb Street Murder' or 'Belgravia Bloodbath' was all over the headlines. Poor Willie Morton was described in terms he would have loved to fulfil, if they had been anything like reality. Wealthy art dealer and smart society gallery owner were not really what Willie was. Now that he was dead, he was getting the sort of publicity he would have had to pay a fortune to get when alive.

Of the Sickert and the Mary Godwin there was no sign. Not a whisper. Eventually, someone came forward and said he'd seen a man sprint out of the back gallery passage on the Lowndes Square side, near Wheeler's, and drive away in a van. No, he didn't know the number nor even the type of van. It was just a nondescript van. The police checked the stock books and the stuff out on loan and the gallery contents. There didn't seem to be anything missing. The Sickert and the Mary Godwin weren't in the records, of course, because Willie hadn't bought them. They were with him on spec. It was odd, though, that there was no correspondence about them, no notes, no appointments or records referring to them in any way. Odd, but not entirely unusual. Willie didn't keep much of a diary and he only had a part-time secretary. The trade were alerted to look out for the paintings and the police put together a sort of Identikit black-and-white picture of them, with my help.

I was described in several papers as the art investment specialist from Jeremy White's. It filled him with glee. The Bank wrung their hands; just the sort of dreadful publicity we don't want, they said. Rubbish, snorted Jeremy to me in his office, absolute rubbish, remember what Somerset Maugham said, don't read it, just measure it. The papers loved the Camden Town Murders angle, especially the Sundays, who played on the idea of evil associations between the painting and the events in the gallery. I was quoted quite a lot and some journalists were suspicious in ways I couldn't fathom but Jeremy said that's just their nasty minds, pay no attention.

The police pumped me and Sue Westerman repeatedly for a description of the assailant, as they called him, not murderer, as we did. It was very difficult. He'd come out of the dark behind me; a gallery without its lights on is a gloomy place, so Sue had only seen him first in outline and, once, a bit more clearly when he lunged at her. He was slender, she said, medium height, lightish hair, perhaps even grey, pale face, clean shaven, and dressed in a brown tweed jacket with grey trousers. That was her lot.

I was even less use. I'd hardly seen him, had fallen under him, had tripped him up in a welter of splintering easel and had got one look at his outline against the back window. That he was lightish or slender I'd have agreed and on his wearing a tweed sports jacket too, but no more. Only one thing stuck in my mind; when we'd grappled together I'd smelt a faint whiff of oil paint or turps or varnish, something connected with paintings or art but hard to define. The police thanked me courteously.

Willie was buried in Fulham cemetery and the inquest was over and done with. No one came forward to claim the paintings. No one reported their theft. I saw less and less and finally nothing of the police. It seemed incredible that a man would kill to take back his own paintings, so they had assumed that they were stolen. Despite the wide publicity, no one came forward to recognize them. After a period of bewilderment, there was a suggestion that perhaps they were fakes. 'It seems unlikely,' I told them. 'Willie claimed they had a really good provenance. Besides, I could understand the Sickert being faked, but why the Mary Godwin? The most they could have reckoned on would be five hundred and on a bad day they might only get two-fifty. People don't risk forgery for that. Willie did say it had its label on, too. He was no fool. They would have had to be damn good fakes to pass Willie and the Godwin would be a stupid thing to fake. I don't see it.'

I had to look through all the Sickert Camden Town Murders recorded. There were quite a few. Sickert was a publicist; he gave titles to paintings after he painted them, not before, like a Victorian artist would. The murder of Emily Dimmock, by having her throat cut, was a sensation, and Sickert, who liked painting the tension implied by two people in a room, particularly the sexual tensions of a dressed man and naked woman, was not slow to use the theme. The accused man, a male model of Sickert's, was acquitted, and the series of paintings bearing the Camden Town Murder captions do not show the actual assassination.

Sickert is what I'd call a Heavy in modern British painting, his life well-documented and written-up by anyone trying to deal with post-1900 art in England. He was prolific, influential, larger than life, married three times in a matrimonially less mobile time than our own, a bit foreign—his father was Danish, his mother British and Sickert himself was born in Munich. His paintings of the pre-1914 era can fetch big money, unlike the post-1918 stuff which used photographs as a base for the surprisingly advanced technique. Critics derided it then but the techniques are now thought of as very modern. Even the pre-1914 work is varied in quality, though, and there is a lot of it about. Which is unlike other Camden Town painters, like Gilman or Ginner, Gore or Bevan, whose work can fetch much more at auction. Mary Godwin was, for me, the square peg in the round hole. Why was the painting by her so important, equally as important as the Sickert to the murderer? I got out a standard reference book, and looked her up. The entry was straightforward:

> Godwin, Miss Mary, (1887-1960) Painter in oil and water-colour of figure subjects, and interiors. Born on 8th March 1887 at Stoke Bishop, Bristol. Studied art at King's College under Byam Shaw 1908-11, under Sickert 1911-14 and Gilman 1915, also at the Westminster Polytechnic. Exhibited at the RA, NEAC, LG, NPS, the provinces and abroad. Lived in Hampstead and died on 23rd February 1960.

Nothing to contradict Willie or Sue in that. Byam Shaw I had always thought of as a Victorian artist. The studying under Sickert 1911-14 was probably at the school he set up with Sylvia Gosse in the Hampstead Road. Her painting was a lighter version of Sylvia Gosse's, not so strong, but Sylvia Gosse is, in turn, a clearer version of some of Sickert's impressionistic blurring. So when would 'The Back Room' have been painted? According to the entry, she exhibited at the Royal Academy, the New English Art Club, the Leicester

Gallery and the National Portrait Society. I got out my record books for the New English Art Club, that break-away society opposed to Royal Academism that Sickert, John, and anyone considering themselves avant garde had belonged to since its start in 1886. The entry for Mary Godwin was short:

GODWIN, MARY, 253 Hampstead Road, NW

1913 S The Landlord (178)
1914 S A Back Room in Somers Town (217)
Paternal Advice (273)
225 Hampstead Road, NW
1914 W Ways and Means (33)
68 Oakley Square, NW
1915 S Mrs Percy Matthias (49)
The Bedroom (91)
Still Life (122)
63, Oakley Street, Chelsea
1915 W. Five o' clock (33)
1916 S La jeune fille (114)
A Back Garden in Chelsea (236)
1916 W Victorian Flowers (222)
1916 S Expectation (2)
The lecture (43)

'A Back Room in Somers Town.' Willie had said the painting was called 'The Back Room.' Or was it 'A Back Room?' 'There's a label on the back,' he'd said.

Looking down the list, I thought that The Bedroom would have been a better title for the painting I'd seen. But Willie had definitely said 'The Back Room.' Could the 1914 'Back Room in Somers Town' be the painting

I'd seen? How the hell did one find out? And why would anyone kill because of it?

'It all seems very strange,' I said to Sue, over lunch at Overton's in St James's, well away from Motcomb Street and the Tate and even Park Lane. It was the first time I'd taken her out to a proper lunch since the one at the Tate about two weeks before. She still looked a bit pale. The events had done nothing for our relationship. Though she'd had publicity as an 'art expert from the Tate Gallery,' it was not exactly the sort of thing she'd wanted. I had rung her up in Hampstead a few times to see how she was and she'd responded well enough to me but without enthusiasm. It had been a horrifying experience. She claimed to be suffering from nightmares. I would have been only too willing to prevent the nightmares or be available beside her to calm and reassure her when they occurred, but somehow her reserve prevented me from suggesting it.

She smiled wanly.

'I mean I can't get to the motive,' I said. 'Even if the paintings had a foreign owner who wanted no publicity, all he had to do was withdraw them, not kill Willie.'

'Please,' she said. 'I've dreaded this. Couldn't you change the subject?'

'In one moment,' I said. 'Just one question. Have you ever heard of a place called Somers Town?'

She looked at me blankly. 'Where?'

'It's called Somers Town,' I said. 'Mary Godwin painted an interior called "A Back Room in Somers Town." Or perhaps it's pronounced Summerstown. Where in hell would it be?'

Her face had cleared. 'Summertown,' she said. 'Not

Somers Town or Summerstown. It's a suburb of Oxford. Summertown.'

'Oxford? Would Mary Godwin have painted in Oxford?'

'She might have. But Camden Town or Hampstead would have been more like it.'

'Of course if it was in Oxford then the superior young man would have been an undergraduate. And the wistful victim on the bed would be a town girl he'd got into trouble or was about to get into trouble. It could be. What a coincidence.'

'What is?'

'Your knowing Summertown from Oxford and living in Hampstead and Mary Godwin knowing Somers Town or whatever and living in Hampstead too. In the Hampstead Road. And the painting having brought us together. D'you believe in chances like that?'

I leaned across the table and took her hand as a waiter brought the lemon soles we'd ordered. She sat quite still and I took it away again.

'Is anything the matter?' I asked her.

'It wasn't the painting that caused our meeting,' she said. 'It was at Geoffrey's in Hampstead. And the Hampstead Road isn't in Hampstead anyway. It runs from Euston Road to Mornington Crescent, west of Euston Station. And when we last met you were telling me that your wife divorced you because you were sleeping with another woman.'

I hardly heard the last sentence. The correction about the Hampstead Road hit me like a blinding light. Mary Godwin had lived, in 1914 and 1915, in the Hampstead Road and then in Oakley Square, NW before moving to Chelsea. Oakley Square is behind Mornington Crescent station—Hampstead Road leads up to Mornington Crescent. Where Sickert and Gere lived.

'Somers Town has nothing to do with Oxford either,' I said, as it all came back to me. 'Somers Town is the area between, roughly, Euston and St Pancras, bounded by Mornington Crescent to the north and the Euston Road along the south. It's not used much as a name for the area now, but I've seen it on street guides. That painting is a genuine Camden Town School painting. So you're right; Hampstead and Oxford are out of it with us.'

Sue nodded. 'So you'll understand—' she spoke softly—'that what with that and your lady friend...'

She left the sentence unfinished. The waiters moved around us, serving lobster and sole, crab and plaice and scallops to wealthy businessmen and Park Lane smoothies out on expenses. My mind went away for a moment as I pondered her implicit rejection of me. You never know nowadays, do you? I mean what they're at, these girls with the new moral codes and boyfriends in their flats, sometimes two or more of them. Three years at Oxford and two at the Courtauld wouldn't leave her an innocent, would they, not nowadays?

She deserved an explanation, though.

'Look,' I said, 'it's like this: the girl I had the affair with, you know, it wasn't serious, it's been all over a long time. It was just the physical thing, well, I mean, you know, sex, I suppose.'

The shadow of a smile came to her face. 'Just sex? But you were married, weren't you?'

'Yes, I was. It started to go wrong because once we had been married for a couple of years, Carol—that was my wife—started to behave as though sex should be on rations or something, like payday, dealt out just once a week in a set time at a set place, in bed and then only maybe. I suppose that was only the superficial sign of something else that was wrong—we didn't seem to have many interests in common and we even argued, badly, about paintings and art—but what could she expect? I mean, it's always struck me that it's odd that a woman will behave one way to attract a man she wants and then when she's got him she expects to drop that and for him to change. How surprised they get when he goes elsewhere.'

'A lot of women would say the same about men.'

She was right, of course.

'Yes, I know, but it was like putting a hungry man into bed with a four course meal every night and telling him he wasn't to eat. In the end he goes out for a bite.'

She burst into a peal of laughter.

'This is deplorable!' She was genuinely rolling with mirth. 'You are the most frightful chauvinist pig I've ever come across! Is that the only way you can think of women? Like a meal?'

I grinned sheepishly.

'Not really. I was mostly brought up by my mother so I do think I'm not quite as insensitive as all that. Perhaps I assumed things about marriage that I shouldn't have. Perhaps. We lived in South America a lot when I was young. My father worked out there. Maybe I picked up a bit of the Latin macho mentality. Grafted on to a rugger-playing Englishman, it can't have increased one's understanding of feminine psychology, eh?'

She smiled at me, still. I had no idea why this cool, rather priggish, Oxford art graduate had induced me to talk about myself like that. Not my image, at all.

'I think you're a hopeless case,' she said. 'Were your parents divorced?'

'Oh no. My father was away a lot. I suppose I admired him from afar as a great, masculine figure.'

'You should have listened to your mother more.'

'Ouch. Yes, nurse. Have you any other patients in your care or can I be your sole charge? Or are you talking from experience? Don't tell me you've been married too.'

Her eyebrows shot up in surprise. 'Do I look like a married woman, already?'

'No. Of course not. But you never know these days. What does a married woman look like? There might be someone, not having bought the full book, a sort of part work, if you know what I mean? After all, you're in your mid-twenties. Why aren't you married?'

She smiled more widely now, in mischief.

'Perhaps because I never found a part-work series I liked enough to get the ring binder for. And I wanted to finish at the Courtauld before all that.'

She made marriage sound, as 'all that', like a hell of a hassle. I changed the subject and we talked about other things because I sensed I'd gone far enough down that line. There was a reserve behind there, something that she was keeping to herself, that I respected. At the end of the meal we parted in real friendship and I put her into a taxi back to the Tate feeling that things were improving.

I tried finding out a bit more from Geoffrey over a

pint of beer at The Shepherd that evening. After all, he'd introduced us.

'Nice girl, isn't she?' he agreed, downing his bitter. 'Friend of Margaret's. Shares a flat with some other girls. Usual sort of thing. Why, what's up? Some other boyfriend in the offing, is there? Or is she still Keeping her Mystery and all that?'

'Very probably.'

'Well, I must say you're being a bit slow, Tim. Should have thought that after all that business in Motcomb Street you'd be providing the strong shoulder to cry on and everything that leads on from there. What?'

Geoffrey Price had been married for eight years and had three children. It's a dangerous condition in a man, apt to lead to fantasies. I bought him more beer.

Sue and the Motcomb Street business were preoccupying me heavily. In my mind I kept revisualizing the two paintings, the one so strong and disturbing, the other more comprehensible, prosaic and sad. I checked with the contacts I had without success. I sat in my room back in Fulham, turning the affair over in my mind. The police were concluding that we had disturbed a sneak thief, that the two paintings on the easel had been removed earlier by someone who wanted no publicity for any one of a number of reasons.

I was sure they were wrong.

The next evening, when the lights flashing by outside the office on Park Lane shone wetly in the cold December evening, my curiosity got the better of me and

I left in the opposite direction from usual, heading for the Northern Line Underground. Just like any ex-consultant, I had to see for myself.

I got out at Mornington Crescent Tube Station, in front of the statue of Cobden, the reformer, and, among other things, Sickert's first of three fathers-in-law. A glance left, towards Mornington Crescent itself, is fairly useless these days, because in 1926 they built the Carreras cigarette factory smack plumb in the centre of the leafy gardens that the Nash-like terrace enclosed. Sickert's lodgings, in No. 6, are blanked off in seedy obscurity behind the howl of traffic along the Hampstead Road and the enormous white Egyptianate block of the Carreras building, now no longer turning out Black Cat cigarettes. It is abandoned to other, more anaesthetic, office and clerical activities. The light that filtered through the slatted blinds of the front bedroom window on to Sickert's Mornington Crescent nudes would be darkened by this building now. And Spencer Gore, Sickert's friend, wouldn't be able, from his window at No. 31, to paint the view of the station across the leafy trees under which he also painted the games of tennis in the gardens the crescent once contained.

I couldn't find No. 225 or No. 253, Hampstead Road. Neither could anyone else. The area has been heavily demolished and Mary Godwin's addresses, like Sickert's various art school buildings, have been swept away and replaced by tower blocks with meaningless names and council apartments in featureless rows of the post-1950s. I suppose one shouldn't blame the architects of the Camden Council or Borough, or whatever it's called now, too much. It was the coming of the railways that buggered the calm, modest, but elegant Georgian architecture of the original town laid out by Lord Camden on the edge of Regent's Park. Three sodding great railway lines and stations, first Euston, then King's Cross, then St Pancras, sliced into the area in the mid-nineteenth century, swallowing up land and spewing out thousands of navvies and tarts and drunken working men cooped into the lodgings that the once-decent houses were warrened into providing. It was a great stimulus to Sickert, who had a real love of low life. A squalid, brawling, seedy, smoky, soot-covered stew of an area with his favourite music hall, the Bedford, nearby in Camden High Street.

It's not exactly an upper-class district now. It was dark and cold as I turned off the Hampstead Road and wandered along Lidlington Place, across Eversholt Street and into what's left of Oakley Square. The pavements rustled with grit and rubbish; walls sprayed with aerosol graffiti about punks and blacks and fuck you, generally or even personally. People coming home from work, irritable, traffic-hunted, shabby, with crumpled plastic carrier bags and brown paper parcels. Bunches of rocky teenagers with violent curiosity took glances at me. My heart sank as I turned into Oakley Square. One side had gone. One old side, where Old St Pancras church was, I mean, replaced by modern cubist maisonette architecture with a backdrop of older, LCC-style blocks of council flats. The centre is wire-fenced off. But another old side was left, a porticoed early nineteenth-century terrace of the Kensington type. Number 68 still stood there, clearly marked.

I leant up against the wire fence across the road

from the terrace and tilted my head back to look. If this was still the same No. 68, Mary Godwin had walked out of that pillared porch on her way round to the Hampstead Road and a short walk to No. 140 down on the left, Rowlandson House, where Sickert and Sylvia Gosse had their school. Or had she? According to the RBA records, she was in Oakley Square at the time of the spring exhibition at the NEAC in 1915. By that time she was studying with Gilman, another founder member of the Camden Town School, who only had four years to go before he died in the 1919 'flu epidemic. But then Sickert and Gilman see-sawed in their teaching at Westminster, so she still might have used the school in the Hampstead Road, where she'd lived so conveniently the year before. I stared at the house, waiting for an answer. 'The Back Room' was a painting of a bedroom. Was it not, more suitably, 'The Bedroom' of 1915? The wallpaper was a bit like the stuff Gilman painted in his interiors, I couldn't remember when. Come to that, I couldn't remember the painting itself that clearly, now. Just the young man arrogantly leaning on the mantelpiece and the girl on the bed. And the sadness of it.

I shook myself. It was colder and darker. A Jamaican was watching me curiously from his parked car. Somers Town was nearby. I went to look for it, to see if there was an answer there, down past the Working Men's College, all Sweetness and Light in Victorian Queen Anne redbrick, she would have seen that. Along into some back street, past a huge ugly block, Godwin Court—was there a connection?—someone had tried to cheer up with New York-style mural paintings, to the Somers Town Family Health Clinic. Then I walked around cleaned-up

Regency terraces opposite a huge low modern school, Sir William Collins, which had obliterated many of the original streets, and where the skin on the back of my neck started to prickle.

I was being followed.

He was slight, slim, quick to move. He was definitely following me. There'd been a few people tramping up behind me as I ambled slowly down the chilling streets that I'd pulled aside to allow to pass. I didn't like them behind me. But they were just people, heading home, to a pub, anywhere. It was the slim, dark shadow, slipping behind a wall or into an entry among the council blocks, that I'd seen once too often. I'd thought it was a boy, a teenager fooling around. But the school is on a straight stretch, Charrington Street, almost in the middle of Somers Town. Smartened Regency terraces on my left, with neat inside gardens behind, clean yellow brick, like it must have been before the railways came in the 1840s. He was behind me there, stopping when I stopped, too much in the open. I kept going.

The road came to a dead end, blanked off for traffic. A wide path continued past bushes into a small park-like area. There was an infants' school, closed. I took a few paces, waiting. On my right was a playground, railed off by a huge fence made of staggered railway sleepers. Very appropriate.

I was in the centre of Somers Town. It was empty.

Whatever throbbing life there had been in that central part was cleared away to a great yawning gap of impersonal playgrounds, paved areas, blank brick walls and slogans left by departed defacers. Away to my left, across empty streets, were the lines leading to St

Pancras, trains clanking metallically. Somewhere in front of me the path led out of the little park into a street, heading southwards towards the bustle of the Euston Road. I was in no-man's-land, a slum conscientiously cleared to leave a gap in the battlefields where houses, blocks of flats and traffic jostled each other. There was no one there. Just a rustle of leaves which made me whirl around. He came at me from behind a low wall with shrubs in it, a foul, lithe figure with distant light catching a glint on the knife that struck at me like a snake as I flung up my left arm to ward off the blow. The blade sliced right through the Crombie cloth of my greatcoat but I had parried it at an angle, so that my jacket and shirtsleeve took some of the force as well. A burning hot line of cut flesh ran down my forearm, stirring me to action. As he drew back his arm like a flash, to strike again, I brought my right fist round in one great flailing windmill hit, a rugger punch, like a primary schoolboy in his first fight. His arm was still drawn back when I hit him, with all my weight behind the lucky strike, connecting with a great hard squelch between his nose and left eye. It saved my life.

His head snapped back and he staggered half-round, wheeling backwards, half-blinded, presenting his right shoulder to me. I leaned over and planted another windmill shot hard down on the place where the neck joined the shoulder, at the side. The knife clattered across the paving slabs. He dropped on to one knee, gasping. Jubilantly, I made a fundamental mistake. Instinctively I was thinking of the knife as my enemy, as the threat to my life, instead of the man. Any commando trainer would have told me to forget the knife, knock the bastard to the ground and boot him half to death with my leather shoes. Not being commando trained, I jumped across the slabs in two strides and bent down, grasping the knife, so that he could kick me, shrewdly and right up under, in the stomach.

The air supply snapped off. Everything went black. I concentrated on holding the knife tightly until some filtered grey light quickly returned, trying to straighten up and pretend I wasn't hurt while warding off the next kick.

It never came. I waited, peering into the bushes, doubled up, leaning on a low wall. He had gone, leaving me winded, with blood seeping down my left arm. Moving carefully, I shuffled down an alley at right angles, past the railway-sleepered playground and along a brick wall towards some lights that got steadily brighter, lights that belonged to a pub built around the 1820s, probably one of the few original buildings left. It was called the Lord Somers. Whoever the hell he may have been.

6

KINDLY HANDS STEERED ME to a seat. Cockney voices called for brandy. A woman tried to stop the blood flowing while police were called, and an ambulance. My legs were shaking. I tried to pay; they wouldn't hear of it. They said it was a crying shame, weeks since anyone had been mugged like that, gave the area bad name, you were lucky, mate, held on to your wallet, did you? They were quite excited; was he black, they wanted to know, and seemed disappointed when I shook my head. Two West Indians further down the bar smiled knowingly.

'Young Irish hooligans, man,' they said. 'Tearaways. From the estates. We know.'

A policeman came in and took me over, calling me sir, solicitously. The friendly London faces nodded and went back to being impersonal, apart, wondering what a man like me was doing walking in the area, but not too curiously. Nothing in London would surprise them much.

I waited in an out-patients' department for half an

hour, oozing blood among a variety of other injured supervised by an uninterested nurse.

After I'd been taped and bandaged up I checked with the police.

'He was following me,' I said.

The constable nodded. 'They often do, sir. Wait till you're in a quiet place. Not many muggers hang around hoping a well-dressed punter will turn up in Chalton Street or the kids' playground, if you'll excuse me saying so.'

'Do muggers come straight at you with a knife rather than demanding the money first?'

'Sometimes, sir. To frighten you. So you'll give them no trouble. Mostly they bash you one first, though; not too much of the knife stuff. Taking a short cut or something, were you, sir?'

I became aware that his interest was more than casual. Well-dressed gentleman getting into knife fights in Somers Town might be involved in interesting activities, perhaps criminal activities. I didn't feel like explaining myself; I couldn't swear that my attacker was anything like the man at Willie Morton's; I decided to go home. The constable put me down as another statistic.

The next day I went to see Sue at the Tate. I bought her a coffee and a sandwich in the buffet this time. My arm hurt a bit and I wasn't in the mood to impress; if she wanted to keep things professional only she could have it that way, I thought miserably. The next big lunch could come in the way of business, when she'd done a job for us. I felt lousy. But she was quite upset.

'You look pale,' she said, 'are you all right? Shouldn't you stay at home or something?'

'No. I didn't lose much blood. I had a pint of Guinness on my way here. Soon build me up.'

She laughed.

'Teach me a lesson,' I said ruefully. 'If you're going to do historical research on art in Camden Town, do it in daylight.'

'I could have told you,' she answered, shaking her head, 'if only you'd asked. The whole area has been three-quarters knocked down and rebuilt in the last forty years. What on earth were you looking for?'

'I don't know. I can't explain. I had to talk to you about it. It doesn't make sense, does it? I can understand that there might be aggro over a stolen Sickert, or a faked Sickert, or whatever was wrong. Quite a lot of money could be at stake. But where does the Mary Godwin fit? She's not big money, is she?'

'I do hate the way you think about art, Tim. You see why I don't like the art market. That poor man got murdered because of it. And you might have been killed, too.'

'And you.'

She shook her head.

'I mean last night. It might—' She bit her lip.

"What?"

'It might be something to do with it. The attack.'

I thought so, too, but I wasn't going to frighten her by saying so. If I was some sort of target because of my presence at Willie Morton's, then she might be as well.

'No. I don't think so. Why wait till last night if it were? He could have had a go much earlier, any time. Why suddenly pick on me when I'm in Somers Town? No, it was an ordinary mugger. The Hospital for Tropical

Diseases is nearby; all sorts of types, seamen and the like, go there for inoculations. Never can tell.'

I patted her hand.

'Camden Borough's famous for its communists. They probably saw a capitalist-looking type and decided to do me in.'

She smiled at that. I began to realize that I was really getting much more attracted to her. There was some barrier that I hadn't broken down, perhaps never would. Ah, was that it? A challenge. Was I still responding like a Boy Scout to the prospect of another achievement badge?

'Look, Sue, I just wanted to ask you again. What chance does one stand of tracing paintings like that? You said that the books on Sickert can't list all his paintings. I suppose for Mary Godwin it's even worse?'

She nodded. 'It's a nightmare. You have to check all the known exhibitions by all the different groups— Sickert was always politicking with different factions, artists being what they are, and arguing about art—and even then you don't necessarily know what a given title looks like. Sickert often painted a picture and then gave it an arbitrary title, afterwards. The Camden Town Murder ones weren't started as that; he liked publicity, so he gave them a startling title, after he'd painted them. And then there are all the paintings that weren't exhibited, just sold straight out or kept until the death of the artist and the studio was broken up. Or lost. Or lent to someone and forgotten. Or swapped. You have to have some sort of background when a painting turns up; sometimes it's a bit tenuous. But then you check the painting for style and technique and background. Those

Camden Town School interiors were often painted in the same rooms, No. 6 Mornington Crescent, say, with the same details, a toilet mirror, things like that. They have to fit.'

'You mean there are still paintings around in people's houses, waiting for discovery?'

'Of course. It's only just started to become a collectable school, outside of experts and specialists. You should know that. It's you who's been getting into modern British art, isn't it? For those who can't afford the French.'

I agreed.

'Would you like another coffee?'

'No, thanks. I must get back.'

'Can we meet again?'

'Why—well—yes, of course. I thought...I mean, you wanted me to look at paintings for you sometimes, didn't you?'

'Yes, I didn't mean that. I meant, you know, otherwise.'

Sue looked down at the table.

'I—I'm a bit tied up until after Christmas, Tim. I'm going home to my parents in Hampshire and then I'll be going skiing.'

'Oh.' I felt a hard pang of disappointment. 'With a party?'

'Yes. Something like that.'

She was still looking down at the table. I gritted my teeth and braced myself. Scrum down, Simpson, don't shirk the issue.

'Look, Sue, if I'm just being a nuisance, that is, if there's someone else and I'm just—well—you know—being a bore—'

Her face, looking up at me now, was softly repentent and concerned, but still with that slight amusement that I seemed to give her.

'You are a strange, old-fashioned man, Tim,' she said. 'But you do go straight to the point, don't you? Yes, there is someone else. Who'll be in the party. I've promised to go. Try and see that. You're not a nuisance. I do like you. Let's meet when I get back, shall we?'

I was out of my depth. She was making me feel like a gauche schoolboy again, after years of thinking I was a big man now. I rallied myself.

'Fine,' I said heartily. 'Let's do that, I'll give you a call after New Year then, shall I?'

'Yes. Well, about the middle of the month, when I'm back. All right? It will be something to look forward to. Something nice. But I must go now—'Bye, Tim.'

And she left me sitting in the bloody buffet staring after her as she walked firmly away, back up the stairs into the building on her soft brown shoes.

I began to wonder what the hell I thought I was doing. Of course Sue would have some other boyfriend or friends. It was ridiculous to suppose otherwise and, by all that she'd said, I was hardly in the most suitable profession from her point of view. A profession which had led her into the fracas in Motcomb Street. Enough to put any girl off. I tried to concentrate on work back at Park Lane over the next week or two. When I travelled to and from the office I was conscious of people around me, apprehensive of being alone in case someone might attack again, but no one did. From that point of view, things started to settle down and I began to feel that the personal aspects of the two attacks had been exaggerated in my mind. Only two events occurred to disturb my steady return to normality. The first was that, before Christmas, two of Sickert's paintings came up for sale in the rooms in one of the last sales before the holiday break. One was a Dieppe scene, painted around 1904, and it fetched about £15,000. The other was one of the Camden Town Murders, subtitled 'What shall we do for the rent?' It wasn't the same as the one I'd seen at Willie Morton's. The woman was on a bed on the left-hand side of the painting, lying back nude in a less revealing attitude. The man was not sitting. He was standing behind the bedhead, in shirtsleeves and the same stiff suit, looking down at her. His pose was much more threatening than the despairing one at Willie's and the juxtaposition of the figures more tense. This painting had a reasonable provenance; descent from some friend of Sickert's, they said, via various galleries. It fetched £23,000.

And then, early in January, Jeremy changed the course of my life for a second time.

7

THE PLANE WAS NOT exactly crowded, because there were only five of us.

The merchant seamen from Liverpool, with labels tied to them, like evacuees, en route via British Caledonian to join a steam packet, coffee-ship or coffin-ship, in Santos.

A bearded, greyish chap in sandals, slightly built and with light grey pepper-and-salt hair, dark glasses, canvas trousers and a bristling hop-sack jacket like those worn by nineteen-thirties intellectuals. He looked as though his ticket had been paid for him by someone like the British Council, in return for lectures to South American audiences on the Meaning of the Agricultural Depression as a Background to the works of Thomas Hardy. Or, perhaps, the influence of William Morris's Wallpaper Designs on the development of modern Socialism? Perhaps.

A rather smooth company director in a shiny Tropicadilly suit and crocodile-skin shoes, slightly foreign-looking, perhaps an Anglo-Brazilian, who disappeared into first class waving his red boarding card at the oily smiles of a poofy steward.

And me.

They couldn't be making much profit on this trip, I thought, as the big jet lumbered off the Gatwick runway and angled itself slowly round into the direction for Rio. Mind you, no one in his right mind goes to São Paulo on a Saturday night in mid-January, that far ahead of carnival time. Sensible people stay at home on a Saturday night with their wives and families. If they've got wives. Let alone families.

'Drink, sir?'

A smartly kilted British Caledonian stewardess, crisply efficient and as friendly as a professional nurse, stood by me. I ordered a large whisky and soda. She nodded approvingly, and served me straight away. Stewardesses like solidly predictable business passengers with no romantic misconceptions. Rather like Tate Gallery administrative assistants, perhaps, I thought, as I pondered over my excursion.

Late one morning I had been standing in my office in Park Lane, looking out of the long narrow window across the busy road to the bare trees in the Park, my hands rammed into my trouser pockets. For the first time in many months, I was starting to take stock of myself.

I was feeling mildly prosperous. When Carol and I divorced, we were lucky that we had no children. She took a greater lump of our combined assets than legally due to her and I let her get away with it out of a sense of guilt. She told me quite simply that she wanted nothing more from me; she would be leaving the country, tired of my absences on business and my insensitive nature and my infidelity. I refrained from retorting that my absences on business were a necessary result of our joint ambitions and that my infidelity stemmed from her own pattern of behaviour. It was a fortunate enough break as it was. When everything was over, I sent her half of the share I had left as an extra bonus and our lawyers drew a double line under the account; neither of us owed each other anything any more. I sometimes wondered where she was and what she was doing, but less and less as time passed by. I began to realize that I was free again, that I was starting to make some money and that one day, quite soon, I would have to decide when to take a holiday and what to do with it. The business at Jeremy White's was going quite well and was interesting. The affair in Motcomb Street had brought some clients we might never have had and, though this source still gave me severe cause for unease, I had been kept busy. Now that there was less pressure, I was able to look around a bit.

One thing I felt was that my personal life was drifting. As an ex-business consultant I was, by habit, a workaholic and I had carried this habit with me into Jeremy White's. I lived by myself in the two-room flat in Fulham I had chosen, at the time of the divorce, for its easy economy. It wasn't great, but it was easy to heat and keep clean. I hadn't anticipated being so much better off and I still felt that things might not last, but I could now afford something better if I wanted it.

My thoughts naturally turned to Sue Westerman. It was like thinking about a large barrier, not a brick wall, but a big friendly attractive hedge of the country sort, with flowers and evergreens and brambles all mixed up in it. And quite impenetrable. Things were ridiculous. As my sense of balance, distorted by divorce and work in the new job, returned slowly to normal, I began to wonder why I still wanted to see her so often. If she had other boyfriends she had kept quiet about them except for the one she was skiing with. I met one or two people who had known her at the Courtauld and they said how pleasant she was, a bit idealistic, but pleasant, and what an awful experience in Motcomb Street...I spent Christmas alone.

It was time I got out more. Met more people. Started a social life. Accepted more of Geoffrey's invitations and went to watch the odd rugger match. Why not?

Jeremy's call had interrupted all that. I went straight to his office where Penny was clearing away a pile of papers and taking last bits of instructions down on her shorthand pad as she left, flashing a quick smile at me.

Jeremy looked at his watch.

'Thank God,' he said. 'It's twelve o'clock. Have a gin and tonic?'

We had an office rule that no drinks came out before midday. Jeremy stuck to it strictly, despite pressures and personal inclinations. I accepted and sat down.

He produced the usual generous measures, came round from the back of his desk with some papers and then sat near me across a small occasional table which had casual chairs round it. None of the across-the-desk stuff. He was looking pleased, a bit excited, and obviously ready to impart information to me.

'I've just come from the Bank,' he said, taking a swig of gin and tonic. 'Meeting with my uncle.'

I raised my eyebrows politely. 'Sir Richard? About this business?'

Jeremy smiled. 'For once he had to be quite polite to me. We've put quite a large chunk of business the Bank's way. One of our private clients turned out to have a business he wanted to expand that depended on tropical hardwoods. I introduced him to the Bank and they've done a double deal, financing him and arranging long-term supplies of timber. Right up their street.'

'That's excellent. Don't tell me we're in the Bank's good books at last.'

He shook his head. 'Not quite. Not yet, anyway. But while I was talking to my uncle something else came up. It turned out that he is rather worried about one of the Brazilian ventures.'

'Ventures?'

'They tried to diversify. A lot of foreign businesses in Brazil have had to. Can't get their money out—exchange control very tight—so profits either have to be ploughed back into the existing business, or put into something new. Well there's a limit to the timber business. Too many eggs in one basket. They've done a bit in beef and tobacco and coffee but we're not a Vestey or BATS or whatever. So they went for more consumer products. After all, Brazil's got a huge population, about a hundred-odd million of them, and they're multiplying fast.'

'A lot of people have lost their shirts doing business with and in Brazil, Jeremy,' I said.

He nodded. 'I know. That's what's worrying my uncle. Apparently they've bought a perfume and cosmetics company in São Paulo and the thing is just swallowing money. Normally, as you may know, the Bank has a few bright young whizz kids with Harvard Business School diplomas that it sends out to sort out that kind of muddle. Well, one's broken his leg skiing down Mont Blanc, another's driven his Aston into a multiple crash on the Ml, doing himself a bit of no good, and the only other one available has got himself locked into Singapore on some timber business that's got into a mess between Lee Kwan Yu and the Malaysians. Very ticklish one, that.'

He finished his drink.

'So naturally, I thought of you. Have another, Tim?'

'Eh?'

'Another drink?'

'Oh yes, thanks. But what d'you mean? You thought of me?'

'My uncle was very dubious at first. To him you're still the Motcomb Street Scandal, I'm afraid. But you were a natural for it. I told him about your background. Perfect. And then the language. That clinched it.'

'The language?'

'Yes. You speak Spanish, don't you? I remember you saying so.'

'Jeremy, in Brazil they speak Portuguese, not Spanish. I speak Spanish.'

He burst into one of his high-pitched roars of laughter and spilt some of the drink he was carrying.

'Oh my God. I am hopeless at that sort of thing. But you can manage, I'm sure. They are similar, aren't they? And most of the people we have there speak English, anyway.'

'For God's sake. What do they want me to do?'

'Go and look at it. Tell the Bank what to do. It'll be a great feather in our cap, Tim. I'm sure you'll have no problem, with your experience. I'll get Geoffrey to keep an eye on your side of things here. You're not tied up or anything, are you? Be an interesting trip, I'd have thought. Stay for carnival in February. Why not?'

Indeed, why not? Apart from the responsibility and the possibility of buggering up relations between Jeremy and the Bank, what was there to stop me? Not Sue Westerman; in fact a bit of distance between me and London might put her in perspective. The art market wakes up again in mid-January after its winter holidays, but two or three weeks' absence from me wouldn't kill the business. A change might be as good as a holiday, even if it were to be a hardworking one. Jeremy's desire to get in the Bank's good books might be helped by me and do us all a bit of good. Perhaps a future career with not just Jeremy, but the Bank itself?

'Delighted to help,' I said, 'if I can. You'll fix things so that I can meet Sir Richard or whoever to agree terms of reference, introductions and so on?'

He beamed. 'Splendid. Of course I will. Oh, splendid. You see, Tim, I knew you'd be an asset. Knew it. You'll go almost immediately, won't you? My uncle's quite concerned.'

'OK.'

He chattered happily about arrangements and meetings and who at the Bank would provide the necessary information and all that sort of thing. So it seemed quite natural when I said to him, casually, 'I suppose I'll be meeting your cousin? The one you were at Eton with?'

His face fell.

'Oh dear. Of course. I haven't ever told you about Luis, have I? Look, we better go for lunch together. You'll find it interesting, actually, but there's a bit of a family skeleton that you'll have to know about.'

And so we ambled along to the Mirabelle and ordered a rather gratifying lunch while Jeremy told me how his cousin was a shareholder in the Brazilian end, but had been excluded from any executive position following a bit of hanky-panky no one liked to talk about that had happened two years ago.

'It's been a bit of an outlaw branch of the family,' Jeremy sighed, as though his hadn't been, 'although one has a certain sympathy, for all that.'

'Oh, really?' I prompted him, in genuine curiosity. Family background might become important for me.

'Well, it started with his grandfather. My great-uncle, I suppose he was. He was the only son of the Brazilian branch round the turn of the century. A bit before the first war he was sent over to London to learn the business at this end. They all were, you know; standard thing. But it seems he was a bit of a hell-raiser—no harm in that—and a rebel. After a few months he disappeared, or just didn't turn up to work, and it took a devil of a time to find out that he'd enrolled at the Slade and had become a typical art student. Still had his allowance and got into a frightfully fast set. Life for a young wealthy Anglo-Brazilian, in Brazil, is a bit different from treadling away in the City. I suppose he wanted a bit of fun. Think of it: London in its heyday with horse-drawn traffic and theatre girls and all that.'

Jeremy helped himself nostalgically to another glass

of Beaune, as though he might have had it better and been more comfortable seventy-odd years ago. I didn't disillusion him and I didn't correct him. There weren't many horses left by 1912.

'Anyway the family got into a tizzy and pleaded and threatened, but by that time he was really head over heels in love with some artist's model and the bohemian life. What really snapped the elastic was that he up and married her. So they cut him off without a penny.'

Jeremy brooded a moment.

'I've often pondered how people shut the door after the horse has bolted. If they'd cut him off straight away, when he left the Bank, he might have been forced back and seen how impractical it all was. To cut him off after he'd married, when he really needed the money, was damn stupid, let alone a bit nasty. He struggled on, trying to paint, and the girl modelled, but it was clearly a losing battle. Then the war broke out.

'It was in August, wasn't it, nineteen-fourteen, that is, and for a while nothing much happened but gradually, no one knows quite how long it took, he must have made up his mind to enlist. Nowadays we'd all say the sensible thing would have been to clear out and go back to Brazil, but he'd fallen out with his father and he was a patriotic Johnny and everyone else was doing it, so we do know that sometime in nineteen-fourteen he was in the army. Eventually he filtered through into the Artists' Rifles and got himself wiped out, somewhere in France, like most of them, in nineteen-sixteen. Body was never found. Actually his name is up on the Menin Gate. And the girl had a baby. Luis's father.

'Well, just like the Victorian melodrama, the family were heartbroken. Shattered. The English main branch had lost one or two and were being stiff-upper-lipped about it, but the father in Brazil was absolutely desolate. His only son. Steamed over with my great-aunt full of remorse and they set about finding their daughter-in-law and grandchild. They found her, too. She was holding on in Chelsea or somewhere like that in seedy lodgings and they packed her up with all his things and persuaded her to come back to Brazil with them and the baby boy. Sensible girl. She knew her chances in London weren't too hot—there were thousands of models and what-have-you about then and she'd no family or money. Her new parents-in-law were obviously not short of a bob. So off she went. Packed up her digs and off. I'm not sure if it was Chelsea actually; might have been Camden Town. No, it was Chelsea, that's right.'

An inkling of a thought came to me.

'Camden Town? Jeremy, your great-uncle, the artist I mean, he didn't have a collection or anything, did he? Of paintings, I mean?'

Jeremy laughed. 'Thought you'd have a nose for that, Tim. Almost certainly not. He was stony broke most of the time. They packed up a couple of trunks of his things and shipped them with them, Royal Mail to Santos and then up to São Paulo. Just his own work, as far as I know, and he wasn't great or, at least, didn't have enough time to become that good. Of course, no one thought much about contemporary art then. Except Roger Fry and similar ilk. Look at Orpen and John and McEvoy. Had to make their money painting portraits of wealthy people. Drank themselves to death. I think we could risk another

bottle of this ourselves though, couldn't we? Toast to a
new era with the Bank, perhaps?'

'If you feel we need an excuse, Jeremy.'

He signalled the waiter.

'Actually—yes, thank you, another of the same—
the girl behaved very well in Brazil. She was quite a
beauty in that sort of voluptuous artists-modelly sort of
way, you know, they like 'em heavyish, don't they, lots of
curves to paint, and she had quite a natural dignity even
if she was a lower-class girl. Quite a hit with the
Brazilian men but she'd been in and out of enough stu-
dios to know about life and the family naturally doted on
the grandchild, so she kept the admirers at a distance
and concentrated on the boy until she died. Quite
young. I suppose her constitution wasn't the greatest,
but there was an outbreak of yellow fever or typhoid or
something in the 'twenties and she died. So the son was
brought up by the family, one way or another. Yes, thank
you, no, just pour it out.'

He took a long swallow of Beaune before ordering
cheese and biscuits.

'Then history repeated itself.'

'How?'

He sighed. 'Luis's father was in his twenties. He fell
for a Brazilian girl and married her. Hot-blooded place,
Brazil. Not approved of by the family at all. They were
livid. Absolutely livid. Mind you, by this time the grand-
parents had died and the Brazilian business was run by
expatriate relatives sent from here. And local professionals where they could get them. But mostly people of
British origin. Lot of Anglo-Brazilian companies run that
way. Like the Argentine.'

'Sure.'

'If she'd been one of the good Brazilian families it would have been different. In fact it would have met with massive approval. Strengthen ties with local wealth and all that. Dynastic stuff. But she wasn't. That's what they couldn't understand. I mean, I gather that a young man needn't go short in that area, what?'

'Jeremy, Brazil is famous for the availability, generosity and obliging nature of its warm young ladies.'

'Admirably put, Tim. Now I see why you accepted with such alacrity.'

I raised my glass to him.

'Well, as I said, history repeats itself. They didn't cut him off exactly but they kept him in a low position in the company. The girl got pregnant. Then war broke out. The second one, I mean.'

'Oh no.'

'Oh yes. We in Britain forget how people flocked to help us. There were thousands of Anglo-South Americans who came over to join up. Particularly from Brazil, Argentina and Chile, although Chile a bit less, I suppose.'

'They came from Chile too. O'Higgins and Admiral Cochrane chucked the Spanish out for them, but Brazil and Argentina had big German influences, as well. Towns in Southern Brazil, Rio Grande do Sul, still have German-speaking papers; hardly speak Portuguese.'

'Well, anyway, Luis's father came across in nineteen-forty, joined up, RAF this time, and got shot down over the Channel. Body never found again. Rather bad luck, particularly on Luis. They sent him over to Eton in the 'fifties. I can't say that he thought much of it; rationing was only just ending and England was like a morgue compared to Brazil. People forget what Sundays were like then; everything closed, church or chapel twice, raining, dreary cinemas. Luis is half-Brazilian, after all. At Eton we used to call him Blanco. Rather funny, that. "Blanco" White, d'you see?'

I sighed. 'Jeremy, blanco is the Spanish word for white. In Portuguese it is branco, with an "r", not an "l".'

He waved that aside.

'Well, it's all the same, Tim. Anyway, what England meant to him was the loss of his father and grandfather with no known grave. A family that was getting distant who had more or less taken over the business in Brazil. He went straight back after Eton and I didn't hear of him for a while. The family rallied round; gave him a job; he tracked about up the Amazon beyond Manaos in the timber business, starting at the bottom. Then he tried the offices in São Paulo and Recife but didn't like them much. Then they sent him over here during the 'sixties and something clicked.'

'The Swinging Sixties?'

'If you like. Personally I never noticed them. Did you? I mean, American journalists and the like kept writing about swinging London, but I thought nothing much of it. Luis did, though. They sent him over for a training course and it seemed as though he'd stay forever. Pile of girlfriends, drove a Jaguar E-type down the King's Road, all the with-it places. Unlike his father and grandfather, he showed no signs of marrying. Still doesn't. Superstitious, he says.'

'Didn't do them much good, did it?'

'I suppose not.' He suddenly brayed with laughter.

'You mean if Luis ever marries, look out for a World War? What a thought. Anyway, in the end, they practically had to frogmarch him back to Brazil. He was here for two or three years. Only came for three months originally. The Bank ended the sort of training job he'd had and told him his next pay cheque would have to be drawn in São Paulo. Bit hard, really. They can always use bright young men and Luis is quite bright when it comes to hardwoods. But they wanted him out there.

'He went back in the end, but not like a lamb. Kept coming back here for his holidays. Can't think why. After all, if you've got a bit of cash I should have thought life in Brazil was much more pleasant than here. Especially if you're brought up to it.'

'You never know, Jeremy,' I said. 'There are people who prefer London. Some of them foreigners. Perhaps some blood strain or another in him, calling for home. Or just the atmosphere. There's a lot to being a slightly foreign young man speaking impeccable English in London. No class barrier. Pretty girls not worried about background, nor you about theirs. Dash of Latin in him. Lots of advantages. You can ignore the general atmosphere of political and economic depression and enjoy yourself because you're not committed to the place.'

'Ah, but that's just it, Tim, dear boy. It may be before your time, but Brazil had a sticky patch in the 'sixties. Looked as though the whole thing was going communist. The generals stepped in and a lot of revolutionary gentlemen and criminals just disappeared. Taken quietly up a side alley and disposed of. Well, Luis got a bee in his bonnet then. He wanted his money over here, or in Switzerland or the Caymans. Just in case. Even though the generals won. Bank wouldn't hear it. That's what led to the trouble. He'd been working away in the São Paulo office for six or seven years after that, all seemed quite well, career progressing, usual thing. Then the Brazilian exchange control authorities came politely round. It turned out that Luis had been fiddling things, not the Bank, but his personal accounts, to get money out. The Bank of Brazil was pretty steamed up. You know how difficult it is to extract money from Brazil. There's a long history of wealthy families out there salting their money away in Europe or the States and the locals hate it— determined to stamp it out. Unless you're a general, of course, then you're different.'

I thought of Willie Morton, arse on desk, finger on nose, telling me the same sort of thing, but said nothing.

'Well, White's Bank had to be seen as whiter than white. What? Offered to remove Luis from all executive power if the Brazilians took it no further. I dare say there were a few personal favours indulged in, too. They agreed, so Luis got the bullet. He still has his family shares in the Brazilian holding company, of course, attends shareholders meetings, but the show is run by other Bank directors and expatriates and the like, as I told you. Luis has always been a bit outside, now he's thoroughly alienated. Opposes the diversification policy bitterly because it means more concentration in Brazil. Causes a shindig at shareholders' meetings. That's why this perfume business is so embarrassing to my Uncle Richard.'

'Poor Sir Richard seems to have quite a lot of trouble with cadet members of the family.'

Jeremy grinned. 'This is a profitable cadet branch.

He'll come round. Especially if we help him a bit in Brazil. It's over to you, Tim.'

After that, I had a rapid briefing in the City, cancelled the milk and papers, and, two days later, was on the plane. It was a smooth trip. I drank more than I should have and stretched out to sleep luxuriously across the centre seats. It wasn't until I got off at Rio that I found that someone had rifled my briefcase.

8

IF YOU'VE GOT ANY SENSE you don't stay on the British Caledonian flight onwards from Rio to São Paulo. The reason for this is that British Caledonian, like other international operators, have to fly to the Viracopos airport of São Paulo, which is only so-called São Paulo really, because it is way out near Campinas, nearly two hours' drive from the city centre. They built it during that great vogue there was in the 1970s for siting big city airports leagues away from the cities they serve.

What you do is get off at Rio and catch a local flight by Cruzeiro to São Paulo's Congonhas airport, which is much closer to the city centre. It's a little wrinkle I had learnt from previous visits and the travel agent in London looked at me respectfully when I demanded that the ticket be made out that way.

It was when I got out at Rio and went through Immigration that I noticed. I always kept my passport, ticket and travellers' cheques in the lid pockets of my Antler briefcase. Their order was changed. I didn't think about it at first, being too occupied with handing over the passport to the checking desk, but when I put it back, in its normal place, the changeover hit me.

I sat down in the transit area and went through the files and papers I'd brought. Someone had been through them. Those bloody seamen, I thought savagely. But the travellers' cheques were still there, untouched. Surely, though, they'd have had the sense to know they weren't going to get away—no, a port like Santos, a good imitation signature, they'd be away on a ship soon. They could do it. But they hadn't.

Out of the corner of my eye, I saw the first class passenger stroll languidly into the area, smoking casually. A regular, I thought. He'll be for São Paulo. There was no sign of the British Council intellectual. He must have got off completely or gone on to Viracopos with British Caledonian. He could even be going on to Buenos Aires. When they called my flight to São Paulo I found I was muttering to myself. On that empty overnight flight there would have been plenty of time for someone to go to my original seat while I was sleeping across in the centre and help themselves. I hadn't even thought of it. There was nothing of real value to an outsider. Some statistics and accounts of the Brazilian organization, with an organization structure, and then figures for the perfume and cosmetics company. Fairly sorry figures they were, too. They were of no value to anyone, unless a competitor, wanting to reassure himself. There was not much about me, either. My passport, of course. My wallet had slept with me. A few investment papers I'd promised myself I'd read in a spare moment and an auction catalogue from the previous year with some important eighteenth-century paintings described in it. There was no reason to bring much else. I wanted to concentrate on the Brazilian business and leave Park Lane affairs alone for two or three weeks.

As we crossed to our flight we were diverted along a passage, away from domestic departures, due to redecoration work. We had to follow a route that led along a glasslined corridor over the international transit area. The British Caledonian flight for Viracopos was reloading its passengers and I saw the two seamen with their tie-on labels trailing down to the departure gate. Behind them came the bearded British Council man, still in dark glasses. As he got to the gate, handing in his pass, he took them off briefly as he flashed a smile at the gate check girl, and I stopped. He was gone, glasses back, away down the entry tunnel and the view had only been momentary, but under his left eye, across the nose, there was a dark smudge, like the remnant of a real shiner that a man has received a month or so before. The British Council man had had a black eye. A black left eye. Just like that bastard in the Somers Town play area would have had after I landed the overarm purler on him that saved my life.

It could be a coincidence. Even lecturers might get black eyes. If he was a lecturer; if he wasn't, what was he? An artistic man, that's what, who'd spent a night in a plane near me while I slept, leaving my briefcase available to him. So, if he were my enemy, and attacker, why was he leaving me now?

I was still perplexed when we landed at Congonhas.

Feelings about São Paulo are not usually very uncertain. It is like a vast Latin version of New York or

Chicago, without the intensity of Manhattan, but with many high buildings and a much warmer climate. For that reason, it is much dustier and more easy-going, even though it is a big, noisy, polluted and high pressure city. You either like it or you don't; there are no half-measures about São Paulo. I like it. I'm a city boy.

Sir Richard had arranged for the perfume company's general manager to meet me at Congonhas. After the years of travelling alone as a consultant, it was a luxury to be met by a chauffeur-driven car and to have Mark Zuridis, the general manager, smiling and extending his hand to me.

Mark Zuridis's file had been lent to me at White's. He was born in Alexandria of a Greek father and English mother. Educated in Egypt until his teens at an English-style public school, then in the States. Some time in the early 'seventies he had come to Brazil with an American wife. She divorced him and left; he hadn't remarried. He spoke English, Greek, French and, naturally, Portuguese. Brazil is very like the United States: people of all cultures, single or mixed in themselves, arrive there and are rapidly assimilated. Within five years they are Brazilians, loving the country and convinced of its great future. Mark Zuridis was no exception. Neither was the train robber, Biggs.

He was a stocky figure in a light grey tropical suit, white shirt and grey tie. Crisp wavy hair topped a broad, suntanned Greek face. He smelt slightly of lavender; in South America, lavender is a fragrance used by men for an aftershave. He smiled broadly and spoke in perfect English.

'Welcome to Brazil. Welcome to São Paulo, Mr

Simpson. Or may I call you Tim? My name is Mark. You know, here in Brazil, we tend to use Christian names a lot; at the factory they will call you Mr Tim, Senhor Tim, just as they call me Senhor Mark. You don't mind?'

'Of course not. How do you do, Mark.'

He smiled happily. I felt sweaty, dirty and crumpled beside him.

His eyes searched behind me.

'You must have travelled with Luis, as I told him.'

'Eh?'

'Senhor Luis. Luis White. He was on the plane with you, wasn't he?'

I suddenly realized that he must be talking about the first class passenger. I felt a complete fool.

'No one told me. I'd no idea. He must have been the passenger in first class. I was in economy.'

Mark's face cleared sympathetically.

'Ah, of course. And White's probably didn't think to tell you, but I heard he was coming back from a visit to England. There was no reason why they should, of course. Unfortunately. But when he travels he still sometimes uses our telex. It is a small service we can still render.'

I felt considerably irritated. I'd been put in my place in the pecking order. No first class travel. Not advised of Luis White's presence in the plane, although Mark had been. Not even an introduction. But then, did Jeremy know? Or Sir Richard? Or had they simply decided to keep me apart from Luis, deliberately? How damn stupid. But Jeremy always said that White's were stuffy.

'Are you meeting him, too?'

'Oh no. He is going on down to Curitiba.'

'Where?'

'Curitiba. A coffee area. Luis has some land and interests there. In a small way, you understand, nothing like the Souza Cruz company, er, that's British American Tobacco to you.'

He was showing off, I thought, still irritable. Showing how he knew the big directors or members of the family and about business. He must have sensed it.

'But you are tired, I'm sure. We'll take you to your hotel right away. I put you in the Oropesa. Is that all right?'

'Of course. It's a first rate hotel.'

As we walked to the car, his man carrying my bags, I felt I'd better make an effort to be friendly. It wasn't Zuridis's fault that the Luis cock-up had occurred.

'Although,' I said, 'as I recall, the Oropesa is a little more conservative and strict about, shall we say, visitors to rooms, than many other hotels here?'

He stopped, looked at me, and then laughed broadly. He clapped me on the back.

'My dear fellow! You have been here before! You are a Paulista, I think? Eh?'

'Well, shall we say, I think Rio is very beautiful but I certainly am more a Paulista than a Carioca. I like São Paulo.'

'Ha-ha! Excellent! I am going to enjoy your visit. So will the rest of the boys—I mean, of course, my management team.'

He seemed quite open and friendly, without any obvious reserve or resentment that the general manager of an unprofitable subsidiary might show at having an investigation from a far-distant head office sent to pry into the reasons for his lack of success. It could have been that his original American background in business might have trained him to accept the overseas parent's auditors prowling round. Most so-called multinationals are, in fact, American companies who control their overseas subsidiaries tightly by means of visiting specialists based in New York, Akron, Topeka, Kansas, or wherever head office might be, who put the local business under a microscope. The old British colonial tradition of giving the man on the spot discretion because of poor communication by galleon is a custom the Americans have never fallen into. In that respect, White's team of visiting bright young men were modern developments for an old City trading company.

As we drove into the downtown area, he gently drew from me how long I had been with White's and what part of the Bank I worked for, presumably to find out which director, Sir Richard or another, I was closest to. The Greeks are political animals. When I told him I was with Jeremy, his eyebrows shot up.

'Jeremy! I've never met him. But he's the—what do you call it?—'

'The personal finance part. Personal investment and tax schemes.'

'Yes, I know, but Jeremy, he's Sir Richard's nephew; I didn't think he was part of the central Bank organization.'

'He isn't. I'm on loan to the bank. I used to be a business consultant.'

His face cleared. I explained the reasons for my involvement and let drop a bit of my background. He didn't miss a trick.

'But that's even better!' His voice lowered diplomatically. 'You know, some of those bright young men at the Bank, clever of course, but they are not very experienced. Now you, on the other hand, with your experience of many businesses, I am sure that you will be able to help us.'

And on he went, enthusiastically, about his perfume and toiletries and cosmetics, saying that the market in Brazil was enormous and he was sure it would be a success, this starting lack of profit was only temporary. With my help, he flattered, they would be able to overcome these passing problems, I would see that. White's had not really understood what they were getting into, how good it would be to have me in London to explain, of course, Tim, you would always be kept in the picture. And now, here in São Paulo, you will get every assistance you need, just say the word, visit anywhere, what sort of programme were you wanting to follow?

We had reached the hotel. My bag was going up to my room. The rifled briefcase was in my hand. Ah yes, the programme. The point at which I established my credentials.

'I'll wash and rest up a bit now,' I said.

'Of course. Perhaps later this afternoon—'

'This afternoon I'd like a first quick visit to your office and factory. I'll spend a few days going through things with you there. Then I'd like to do some store checking, market research stuff.'

'Ah yes. We have got some market research information, not very detailed, but the normal sort of thing.'

'I'm sure. But I'll want to look myself. Department stores, supermarkets, the normal outlets, pharmacies, I guess, whatever.'

He put his hand on my shoulder.

'This is tremendous. This is most welcome. I am sure we can work together well. You will see what my team has achieved. We are proud of it. White's have sent us a real professional, I can see. But let me hold you no longer. I will call back here at, say, three-thirty?'

'That'll be fine,' I said, briefly. I didn't like that sort of obvious flattery. And, tired as I was, I was nagged by new thoughts that kept coming to me. If Luis White was outside the normal executive routine of White's Brazilian organization, and he violently disapproved of their diversification policy, especially into perfume, why was he using Mark Zuridis's telex service? And why had he not introduced himself to me? If Zuridis had really advised him that we were travelling on the same flight, there might be some other reason for not making himself known to me.

I got into the lift. The operator pressed the button.

'The plot thickens,' I said to him, in English.

Of course, he didn't understand a bloody word.

9

São Paulo is the fastest-growing city in the world. Its ten million population swarm around it like insects, multiplying and attracting more and more to its vast industrial expansion. Around it, in São Paulo state, more towns and cities expand and mushroom up from nowhere, trying to decentralize out to places like Campinas, São Jose des Campos and other Brazilian versions of Milton Keynes. It is warm, diverse, colourful and cheerful. Quite apart from the original Portuguese, then the Spanish and the negro slaves, Brazil has been colonized by Germans, Italians, Poles and Japanese. In their quiet way there have been a few British about, too, though they would not think of themselves as immigrants.

Whenever I used to think of São Paulo, I thought of aquamarines. There is not much that is aquamarine about the city itself, except the sky sometimes, for the daytime colours are white, grey and sub-tropical green, with glimpses of that red soil, terra roxa, like Devon's, that the whole countryside around turns up. Red soil and shanty cultivation outside; a mixture of lower residential areas like the older verdant district of Jardims, gardens, no longer so smart, and high-rise modernity in separate new developments. There's not much that is aquamarine about the downtown shopping area down the Avenida Ipiranga either, where the shoppers jostle on the crowded hot pavements, beneath cluttered modern blocks, and you buy fossil stones with fish imprinted in them from aeons ago, and dried piranhas with nasty savage teeth. It is around there that the gemstone dealers abound, selling every kind of stone that you can think of.

My father sent my mother an aquamarine in 1940, when he was caught in South America by the outbreak of war. She often wore it and showed it to me. He bought it in São Paulo, somewhere near the Oropesa, and when he was in Rio he gave it to a sea captain who put it in his pocket, all fifty pounds worth of it, and sailed his dirty British tramp ship through the torpedoes back to Liverpool. Fifty pounds was a lot of money then. When the sea captain got to Liverpool he put the clear blue jewel in an envelope and posted it, ordinary post, to my mother, who got it the next day. It never occurred to my father or the sea captain that it might not arrive.

It was a long time ago.

I leant up against the window-frame of my cool, air-conditioned room and stared down the long avenue, the Ipiranga, stretching away down past the plaza to the valley overlooked by old Government buildings in classical colonial style. Perhaps Luis White's father had gone to England on that same ship, before the time when hotel rooms were air-conditioned. That man, conceived in a room somewhere to the north of Euston Station by a father he would never have seen, went back like a homing bird to a place where he might have been schooled but where he never belonged, to help beat off the big vultures that wheeled in Kentish skies. My own father got back a year later; by that time Luis White's father was dead, somewhere in the English Channel.

It's inappropriate, I thought irritably, to dwell on the past like this. We British are absurd. In a hot, bright, fast-developing country with an inflation rate of one hundred per cent, no one wants to give a stuff about the past. Give a Brazilian employee a rise in salary and he or she rushes out and hocks it, right away. The increment is mortgaged instantly for something concrete like a new car, clothes or domestic appliances. Everything is for now and the future. Brooding on the past and on old wars is for fools; yesterday's money is fools' gold; life in South America is one of applied hedonism, now, until the money runs out.

The phone rang. I tore myself away from the window.

'Mr Simpson? *La senhorita Nadia em bas.*'

'Eh?'

The clerk's voice was replaced by a throatier, feminine one, with that slightly nasal twang that Brazilian Portuguese gives to pronunciation.

'Senhor Tim? I am Nadia Rodriges. Mr Mark sent me to pick you up—I hope I am not too early?'

'No, no, that's fine. I'll be right down.'

She was waiting in the lobby, apologizing for Mark Zuridis who, she said, had got caught up in a meeting. She was quite a big, attractive woman, in her late thirties, I would guess, sunburnt and widely-built, with dark hair flecked with blond-dyed strands in the current fashion. Brown eyes were set wide in a handsome face with a full upper lip. She held my gaze boldly and frankly, extending her hand, warm and dry, to clasp mine.

'Are you his secretary?' I asked her, as we walked across the tree-shaded street to the inevitable Volkswagen she had parked on the opposite pavement.

'Well—' she walked with her head held up, a firm stride—'yes. Actually I am the general secretary of the company, you know, and Senhor Mark's assistant, what do you call it, a PA, I suppose.'

I nodded as we raffled off to join a hundred more Volkswagens streaming along the Consolação.

'I'm glad you speak English. I'm afraid I'd be pushed in Portuguese.'

She laughed and gave me a full, appraising look. 'You don't speak foreign languages?'

'Only Spanish.'

'Aw, well, then you have no problem here. You can speak, can't you, with us?'

'No, I can't. You can understand my Spanish, but I'll have much more difficulty understanding you. It's always the same with Spanish and Portuguese. The way you blur all your words, slush them about, it's confusing. For example, if I were directing you in this car, telling you to keep straight on, I might say in Spanish, *siempre en frente* and you'd understand me. In Portuguese that would be written *sempre em frente* and it should be easy for me, but in fact you'd pronounce it *semp'em french* and I'd be lost.'

She laughed out loud, then, and wagged a finger at

me. 'Not me, I wouldn't. I'm a Paulista. You've been mixing with Bahianas, I think, Senhor Tim, haven't you? You've been here before.' I smiled.

'I've never been to Bahia. Except on a passing steamer.'

'You wouldn't have to, São Paulo is full of Bahianas, girls from the north-east, you know.'

I nodded and watched the city scatter past the window. She drove competently, her strong legs braking and de-clutching the old-fashioned Beetle. Half the cars in Brazil were Beetles then, taxis as well, careering along the dual carriageways until we branched off, under a viaduct, along a river's edge, wide, with factories and junkyards along it. The high buildings gave way to single storeys and the kerb disappeared from the edge of the road, leaving red-brown dust and rubbish to take its place. We clattered along lumpy asphalt streets until there was a sudden widening again and new roads, laid out in neat squares, proclaimed a recently-built development. She pulled up in front of a long, low, white office block with a newly-watered garden in it. There was a factory block behind. It had been pleasant to defer responsibility on to the lady for a while, to be driven without knowing where and without inquiring. I wondered where Mark Zuridis was and whether the chauffeur-driven car was with him. What rating of importance did I get now, sending his secretary to pick me up?

She seemed to read my thoughts. 'Senhor Mark is at the Bank. They called him at lunch-time. He will be back soon. Please, come in.'

She took me through a marble-floored lobby into a

reception office and through to a large, panelled office with a desk made of jacaranda and photos of Mark Zuridis at various ceremonies on the walls. Here he was opening a building; there at a reception; there with four pretty beauticians in front of a perfumery counter. She ushered me to an armchair.

'Please have a seat. Would you like some coffee?'

'I'd love some. It's what I came to Brazil for.'

She smiled and went out. Her manner now was more impersonal, professional. When she came back it was with another girl, much younger, dark, carrying the coffee. Evidently the Senhorita Nadia was too senior for coffee-making.

'This is Gladys.' She pronounced it glads. 'Senhor Tim, Gladys.'

'How do you do, Gladys.'

I kept my face serious, but pleasant. The sight of a dusky girl, coffee-coloured and attractive, with the improbable name of Gladys made me bite my lip. Nadia looked at me ironically.

'Gladys is a Bahiana, Senhor Tim.'

'Really? From Bahia?'

Gladys dimpled prettily. 'Não. Fortaleza. I am from Fortaleza.'

'Good heavens, isn't that much further north than Bahia?'

'Aw, yes, but you know we call anyone who comes from Bahia or further north a Bahiana. It's a general word.'

'Would someone from Maranhão be a Bahiana?'

'From São Luis, you mean? Maybe. Not really. It's too far. Why?'

They showed little interest. It would be of no stimulation to tell them that the Marquis of Maranhão in the nineteenth century was a bloodthirsty, aristocratic, ex-Royal Navy frigate captain whose real name was Thomas, Lord Cochrane, Scottish son and heir of the Earl of Dundonald, and that he took the title in return for helping the Brazilians drive off the Portuguese in the same way that he had helped the Chileans drive out the Spanish. It didn't work for him with Brazil as it had with Chile, where he is still publicly honoured; in Brazil political wrangling destroyed his scope for action and he never got paid the mercenary money he had been promised. He came back penniless. There was a lesson there, somewhere, but that sort of history is of no interest to modern Brazilians.

'Just curiosity. Historical curiosity.'

Gladys nodded and beamed, then left respectfully. I became aware that Nadia Rodriges was much more than a secretary. She exuded both competence and confidence; I wondered what her relationship with Zuridis could be as I drank my coffee.

She sipped hers and pulled a face. 'I'm sorry,' she said, 'this is not good coffee.'

'It seems OK to me,' I said, surprised. 'I haven't had one of these small, strong, pure Brazilian coffees for ages. It wakes you up and gives you a bit of energy.'

She smiled; the heavy upper lip curled slightly. 'I like good coffee. But it is not good for me to drink too much of it.'

I refrained from asking whether her health was not strong. She looked much too robust for hypochondria. She was looking at me again. 'Will you be staying long in São Paulo?'

Was she pretending she didn't know? Surely nothing in this factory escaped her?

'I don't know. About two or three weeks. Or as long as it takes. But about two or three weeks should be enough.'

'Then you should stay for Carnival.'

I felt myself defensively resenting the notion that I had timed my visit to coincide with such a festive occasion. My work ethic again.

'I'll see. Of course it would be nice, but work comes first.'

She ignored that preposterous idea.

'Really you should go to Rio. The Carnival here in São Paulo is very good, but Rio is the more famous and extensive one.'

I nodded absently, and got up to look at a showcase full of products that were part of Zuridis's range. Bottles of perfume and colognes standing on their packaging; jars of cream and aftershave, nail varnish and eyeshadow. It cheered me up. After dealing with the dead products of a bygone age, no matter how beautifully made or painted, there is something infinitely stimulating in being involved with production now, the manufacture of things people buy for immediate use. The world of art and antiques, I reflected, is like a huge rubbish heap combed by scavengers for valuable castaways.

So what did that make me?

10

I first met Luis White in the boardroom at White's offices in Santo Amaro. I had been explaining that the only thing wrong with the business that Mark Zuridis ran was that it lost money. Otherwise everything was fine.

It didn't go down well.

Mark Zuridis did all the right things. He kept good accounts, promoted new lines, tried fashionable packaging designs, ran a tight sales force and kept distribution costs low, especially for a company that had to sell to places as far apart as Manaos and Porto Alegre. My internal checks hadn't turned up anything obviously wrong. I said it all to the directors I had met, along with Mark Zuridis, after we'd been shown in. The office suite was in one of the newly-developed areas of the city, resplendent outside in aluminium and marble. Inside, the boardroom was panelled in a darkish Brazilian hardwood and portraits of sober-looking members of the White family, none of them like Jeremy, looked down from the walls. While we had been waiting in the anteroom, I had read copies of The Times, Financial Times and the Telegraph, none of them very out of date. It was all very English in a slightly fustian way.

Sir Richard had been quite clear that I was to report to his appointees after my first week. 'No point in wastin' time with a lot of meetin' and greetin',' he'd grunted. 'Get straight down to it and talk to 'em when you've got something to say.'

There were three of them. An oldish, white-haired general manager called James White, sitting in the centre and obviously the chief. I wasn't sure of his exact relationship to the family but he was clearly the closest. To his left, younger, but equally serious, was Peter Lewis, a dark Celtish-looking man with blue eyes, whose mother had been a White. And on his right was a typical Scots accountant with half-moon spectacles, ginger-haired, called Graham Thorburn, not a member of the family. All three spoke with the cultured voices of well-educated Englishmen, even Thorburn, whose origins must have lain well to the north of the border.

It was odd to think that they were all Brazilians, second and even third generation.

'Then why,' James White was asking, somewhat testily, 'is the damn thing not making any money? Eh? We've had to fund another thumping loss this year, you know.'

It was just at that point that Luis White walked in.

Despite the fact that I felt I knew him from the photos on Zuridis's walls and my view of him on the plane, it was a shock. There seemed much to cover up; I knew a lot of it from Jeremy's family lecture in the Mirabelle and, in a way, the knowledge clung within me like a guilty secret. Not only that, he had a lot to explain to me. At close quarters he was not so dark in features, just very sunburnt. He dressed much less conservatively than the others, in a light beige tropical suit and shoes with a basket-weave effect that are not the approved choice of a traditional Englishman, although an Etonian has a disregard for convention. His shirt and tie, however, were straight Jermyn Street material. What surprised me was that the others seemed to be expecting him and showed no consternation at his entry. I was introduced to him in quite urbane fashion by Peter Lewis.

'I think we have seen each other before,' I said, taking the bull by the horns.

'My dear chap, I am most awfully sorry about that.' The voice was cultured, with a good deal of charm. There were inflections of Jeremy but no potential for the ebullient, rapid, almost hysterical laughter that Jeremy produced. He was quieter, with brown eyes, slim and narrow-faced; his handshake was firm and cool. 'For some reason our London end didn't tell me you'd be on the plane. We could have had a noggin together. I really do want to talk to you about Mark's business, now that I have a personal interest, but I had to go on down to Curitiba and I've just got back.'

I wondered why he was lying and thought of my briefcase.

He turned to the others. 'James, I do hope you'll forgive me. The usual sorts of delay, I'm afraid.'

James White nodded and indicated a chair. Luis sat down. Peter Lewis, seeing the perplexity I must have shown, turned to me. 'Mr Simpson, perhaps I should explain. Luis here is, of course, a stockholder in our holding company but for various, er, reasons is not involved in our financial investment side. We've had some discussions with him recently about his role in our activities. I don't think he would deny that he's been rather, er, critical of some aspects of our policy, especially diversification. However, more recently, he has come round to, well, what shall we say, Luis? A broader view?'

Luis White smiled at his relative in perfectly friendly fashion, then turned to me.

'It hasn't been what you might call a vision on the road to Damascus, exactly, Mr Simpson, but I do believe that the toiletry business ought to be right for Brazil and I do see, now, that we have no option but to diversify here. The money has to stay here. It may be that the British Government will one day force British companies to do the same, instead of letting them put up factories in Singapore and everywhere else but the UK.'

He smiled a knowing smile.

Mark Zuridis cleared his throat and looked at me, trying to keep sheepishness out of his features.

'Tim, we have always felt at the factory that Luis could add a great deal to our operations and expertise. I particularly value his addition to the perfume company board for his advice and, of course, additional links with the holding company.'

You snake, I thought. You perfect bastard. You spring this on me now. Why? Why the hell didn't you tell me before? And why are you, the most egocentric, territorial, tree-peeing kind of Greek, happy to invite an intruder, a rival, a family baron into your little lair? That was what your meetings were about, was it?

James White cleared his throat irritably. 'Yes, that's it, Mr Simpson, um, Luis has been coopted on to the board of the perfume company, so perhaps you'd just recapitulate for him, would you?'

I glared at him balefully.

I was bloody livid.

To be on trial was one thing. I realized that. To Sir Richard and his cohorts I was some little man that Jeremy had dug up, a ferret to do some ferreting, and, probably, not very good at it. To them I was not even one of the wankers from the City, but from Jeremy's suspect outfit, knowing sweet FA about Brazil. So I didn't expect to travel first class like a company director. I didn't expect to be given the VIP treatment by White's of Brazil when I arrived. I supposed I accepted, grudgingly, the condescension of James White's attitude. He was an old fogey. Finished. If you work for other people you have to be prepared to swallow their shit. Up to a point. What really made me mad was that this Luis affair had been all fixed up quietly without anyone telling me.

I became aware that my silence and stare at James White was causing an awkward atmosphere. Mark was looking defensive; Luis still half-smiled at me; the others were waiting.

'I take it,' I said, with the weak pomposity of the little man whose position is totally undermined, 'that Sir Richard knows all of this.'

James White raised his eyebrows. 'Of course.' His tone was proprietorial. 'I spoke to him the day before yesterday. On the phone. He agreed. Said it wouldn't affect your work in any way. Does it?'

Back in your place, ferret.

Thorburn was looking at me over his half-moons, a look in which sympathy and expectation were nicely blended. Go on, lad, it seemed to say, forget it. Just go on. I gave Luis a brief summary of what I'd told them.

'Strange,' he said. 'Brazil has, after all, a good many hewers of wood and drawers of water. We have to keep them employed. James and Peter here—and Graham, of course—like me, are not manufacturing men in a detailed sense. We know little of the perfume and toiletries as a business, either. So we thought, since they are very occupied, that I might take a closer interest. A much closer interest. Basically we've agreed that my appointment is executive rather than non-executive. I shall be closely involved. Which is why, in a way, I'm rather disappointed by what you've said. I was rather hoping—we all were, including Mark here—that you'd tell us there was something clear-cut which we could do.'

They were putting me on the spot. First, I had to digest this new turn of events. Secondly, I was, clearly, regarded with considerable reserve. Thirdly, I was a long way from home, playing away on the home ground of these five men. Not that front row forwards of rugby teams are too bothered about that.

Old James White was getting impatient.

'You can speak out, Simpson. We've all agreed that Luis here should get stuck in. He's been away long enough. Now then, I'll repeat my question; why the losses? Eh?'

Ball coming in left, chaps. A nice clean heel out, now.

'Volume,' I said. 'Sales. There's an optimum size to any business and it's always much bigger than you think.'

Thorburn looked at me approvingly over his half-moons.

'You have a nice little operation which could handle much more business. That's one thing. The next thing is that the success rate, or rather failure rate, of products is alarming. It's giving you stock returns, remainders, what ever you want to call them, of astronomic proportions.'

Thorburn took off his half-moons and began to polish them, with even more approval in his manner.

'You launch products all the time. Some of them don't sell. You have to take them back to keep the trade happy. Can't have shops full of dead stock, can you? Gradually you accumulate remaindered stock. Every year you have to write it down, dispose of it. It's killing your profits.'

'You mean—' Luis was keen—'that our products are all wrong?'

'Possibly. Probably. Some of them, anyway. It seems strange, because Brazil is the classic kind of Latin market, with high consumer usage.'

'So what's wrong?'

I smiled at him modestly.

'After one week in São Paulo, I'm not an expert on the Brazilian market. Not yet. That comes in next week's report. Shall we say same time, here?'

I leant forward over the table and fixed James White with my eye.

'Or would you rather meet at the factory? Where it's all happening?'

He didn't flinch.

'Here,' he said shortly. 'We'll meet here, same time. If that is all you can give us for now, that is?'

'That's all for now, Mr White.'

Initiative regained. Up to a point. There was nothing more they could do. A consulting company would take weeks and charge them thousands. James White was implying that I hadn't done much in a week. Mean old bugger. They started to break up and were tuning to go when Luis stopped them in their tracks.

'You and Mark will join us for lunch, won't you, Tim?' Mark opened his mouth and shut it, looking at me. I hadn't missed anything. Not the use of my Christian name, nor the fact that I wouldn't have been asked without Luis's intervention. I smiled at him.

'How kind. I'd be delighted.'

No, not just to put old James's nose out of joint. I wanted to get close to Luis and I had a feeling this was a chance. He relaxed sunnily.

'They do quite a good buffet in the directors' dining-room, don't they, Graham?' he grinned, walking alongside Thorburn. 'We should introduce Tim to some Brazilian dishes.'

'Of course. How do you like São Paulo, Mr-er-Tim?'

We were walking down a corridor to an open area, where I could see a buffet lunch laid out and two white-coated men hovering respectfully. Large picture windows gave a view over a canal, the Rio Pinheiros, I think, and houses, office blocks, dusty roads.

'I like it,' I said. 'I've always liked it. I find the feeling of growth exciting. Not only that; the food and the culture and the people.'

Peter Lewis looked at me, surprised. 'You're an admirer of the Latino, Tim?' He made it sound like a strange aberration, in the way that one fond of Wagner might examine someone's addiction to Jelly Roll Morton. We were standing at the buffet, now.

'Yes,' I said. 'I like people whose feelings I understand. Orientals are the most difficult. Northern Europeans the most implacable. The Latins let you know what they think.'

'Really? Oh, look, do have a drink? Gin and tonic?'

I hesitated, just a fraction. 'I think if you don't mind, I'll have a caipirinha.'

The white-coated attendant grinned in pleasure. James White looked horrified.

A caipirinha consists of cane spirit, called caçhasa or pinga, mixed with lemon, ice and sugar. It is very cooling.

'You like that stuff?' he inquired, with genuine curiosity.

'Yes, I can drink gin and tonic any time in London. When in Brazil—'

Luis turned to Mark with a grin. 'What have you been doing, Mark? Introducing Tim to local Brazilian ways?'

'No, really, not me. I don't know where he got that taste from, I'm sure.'

I took the drink from the attendant, who passed it to me with a flourish. Luis was watching me more closely now.

'You've been here before, I believe, Tim?'

Just like Nadia, I thought; the same remark, almost the same words. Had she told him? No, he'd been in Curitiba all week, he said.

'Yes,' I said casually. 'A few times, when I was consulting. Do you have interests in Curitiba?'

He was quite relaxed.

'Oh no. My mother has retired there now. We always had a place outside the city—a coffee plantation—not very big, but the old house was a sort of country place. My grandmother lived there, years ago. Why do you ask?' His grandmother, the would-be model, saved from Chelsea squalor with her baby, who became Luis's father. Did they put her out there to grass, away from the English snobbery of São Paulo expatriate society, because of her lowly origins?

'I'm a bit surprised,' I said. 'I thought Curitiba was mainly Italians, Poles and Germans. Although, of course, there was a railway terminus there, wasn't there? A repair yard, that sort of thing.'

He nodded, looking curiously.

'Yes, there was. And it's the centre for Parana state, which is a big coffee area. Have you been there?'

'No. But my father was there, in nineteen-thirty-nine. He was a railway engineer.'

They all showed interest, then.

'On the São Paulo line?'

'No,' I said shortly. 'Argentina. He was only visiting as a technical specialist. He was mainly with the Buenos Aires and Great Southern.

Old James White's face lit up. 'Ah, the old BA and Great Southern! That was a line. Down to Patagonia, eh? Well now, no wonder you're an old Latino fan. Here, have another drink. Were you brought up in BA?' I shook my head. 'Just after I was born Peron nationalized the railways. In nineteen-forty-eight. My father lost his job. He tried various others, wandering around South America while we were mainly in England, partly out here. We never saw much of him. India had gone and most of the South American railways too. Twilight of Empire. He died in Peru. I'm afraid that like many British railway engineers, Trevithick and Stephenson among them, South America didn't do much for my father.'

There was a silence. I caught Luis White's eye. For the first time, I saw on his face a look of utter vulnerability, a softness and weakness that he hadn't so far disclosed. He put a hand on my shoulder.

'Well,' he said, 'my position is the reverse, my dear Tim. I'm afraid England didn't do much for mine.'

There was a moment's embarrassed silence. Then we started to choose our lunch from the dishes on the tables.

11

I SAT IRRITABLY IN A HALF-EMPTY churrascaria, chomping my way through steak, chops and chorizo sausages with salad and chips. From time to time I downed a half-litre of German-style beer. Every time my plate emptied or the glass was drained, they filled it again. The south of Brazil, called Rio-Grande do Sul, is just like Argentina and Uruguay; wide open pampas inhabited by the heaviest meat eaters in the world. The churrasco is an Argentine affair, but the Paulistas have enthusiastically adopted that system of an asado, or barbecue-style restaurant, with a fixed fee, in which you can eat yourself stupid on meat.

Observers might have noticed that I was muttering to myself.

After our lunch at Santo Amaro, Zuridis and I had gone back to the factory. Luis White made excuses and left us. I found him difficult to fathom. Like many people who are a cross of two powerful cultures, his character was elusive. The Eton background was not prominent; if it ever had been, it was now submerged beneath a sophisticated South American veneer. The voice and accent were undoubtedly those of a cultured Englishman but the Brazilian half of him, and the day-to-day use of Portuguese and South American idioms, had altered his grammatical construction. Latin phrasing crept into his speech. This was nothing new; even old James and Peter Lewis did it. Years of expatriate life result in a form of colonial English which has its variants all over the world.

Yet Luis White was still very English in some inde-finable way. It was as if he made certain assumptions about himself that one had to accept, even though his other, Brazilian, half was only too evident. He spoke, for instance, like a man to whom London is known inti-mately. There were times when I felt we were not in São Paulo and that he had just popped in from a flat in Kensington to join us. At other times he spoke of the Brazilian interior, beyond tropical Manaos, or down south in cattle country, with a wistful enthusiasm that all Brazilians proudly evince.

The others clearly regarded him as different. There used to be a system in British companies, all over the world, of keeping expatriates on a different plane from locally-employed people, even if those people taken on locally were in fact British. The system in India is full of such examples. Luis was one of them.

What made me laugh quietly to myself was that James and the other two were, actually, not expatriates but Brazilians, even if they were of British stock. The difference lay in that Luis was half-Brazilian by blood, not just by birth; therein lay the start of a whole caste system. Luis showed evidence once or twice of trying just a little too hard to impress and to distance himself a bit from Mark Zuridis. Yet there was a relationship of some sort between them, an unspoken bond or liaison which I felt rather than heard.

I was, of course, bloody livid with Mark Zuridis. He was guilty of plotting without me. In the back of the car he nervously had a try at mollifying me.

'Tim, I am glad everything has gone so well. Luis was very pleased. I really want to thank you. Really. You have been very kind about my organization, most kind in your report to the directors. Everyone has worked very hard and we are proud of what we have done. You and I, I knew we would work well together.'

'I only told the truth as I've seen it so far, Mark. More than you have done to me.'

'Tim! I do not understand. You are upset—about Luis, perhaps?'

'You know bloody well I'm upset. Why didn't you tell me Luis was joining your outfit?'

'It was confidential. Really. I am sorry. Only at the board meeting was it to be official. Until then I was not allowed to say anything. I would like to have, believe me. You have helped us and you are absolutely honest in your report. I am ready to accept anything you say. You know that. But you are not one of the directors. I will provide any facilities you need, but I had to respect a confidence. Surely that does not upset you? I am sorry if it does.'

Methinks he doth protest too much, I thought. Why was I so piqued? Just because they'd treated me like an outsider, or an opposing team member, game to be outwitted? Something to do with Luis, perhaps, and his avoidance of me on the flight? I was angry because he had suddenly been thrown into the arena of the perfumery company, like a new contender, without anyone thinking me important enough to advise in advance. That was it. Simply the treatment as an insignificant company technician, doing a—what was it Jeremy called it?—a pipefitting job.

Mark was rabbitting on.

'Tim, Tim, tomorrow evening I am giving a small party in my apartment. Just casual, you know, as we are here in Brazil. Please will you come? I regret I cannot entertain you this evening, I have family matters, but tomorrow I would be glad to see you. Just some drinks and some typical Brazilian dishes. Perhaps a feijoada— you know it—bean stew with meat. A little music. We Paulistas love to dance. Eh?'

No one from White's had invited me out. I guessed that ferrets, when sent from London headquarters for insertion in local rabbit holes, were left to look after their own red-eyed amusements. I accepted with as much grace as I could muster, and spent the afternoon working bad-temperedly at the factory. The sensitive Latin characters around me moved out of range; even Gladys, from Fortaleza, changed her normal cheerful curiosity to a respectful silence.

The churrascaria was near the hotel. Its glaring lights shone on empty white tables and the waiters were Italians and Argentines. They heaped food on my plate and rolled their eyes at my muttering.

'Tedesco,' said one Italian to an Argentine, who nodded 'Aleman' in agreement. I glowered and tried to look suitably Teutonic for their ill-judged assessment of my nationality. I was very full when I left. Strolling back to the hotel, I drew deep breaths of the warm night air. Not far away, it occurred to me, down the street called Mayor Sertorio, there were pavements and bars where you could choose anything from a coal-black negress to a Scandinavian blonde if you felt so inclined. It had been a long time and I was feeling a lot of self-pity, but I was much too full.

Thinking of the work to be done in the morning, I retired to a fitfully dyspeptic and dream-infested bed, on which images of Luis, Mark, old James and an alluringly naked Gladys got hopelessly intermingled.

After breakfast, ignoring the papaya, which I've always found sickly, I got down to work. Street markets, supermarkets, department stores, pharmacies, chemists' shops, even groceries. Discount stalls were what I was really after. I walked, took taxis, tramped down aisles, until my feet ached and I was hot. Every now and then I had a small pure sweet coffee, strong as brandy, to jolt back the energy and digest last night's meat.

At three I got back to the hotel, drank a large cold beer, showered and went to bed. I guessed I had found where Zuridis had scope for cheating and even, possibly, where Luis might have caught up with him. It made me sleep soundly until six.

Mark Zuridis's flat was quite large, in a block not far from the Via Augusta, the once-fashionable shopping street in Jardims. The party consisted of a few managers from the factory, their wives, and a smattering of others connected with the business. Luis wasn't there. Nor, to my regret, was Gladys, with whom I had dream-inspired thoughts of progress being made. Clearly she was too lowly for this. A hi-fi played sambas; the buffet was loaded. Mark greeted me effusively and introduced me all round. He seemed very cheerful and confident, which nettled me again. I accepted a very large iced whisky and soda. I had talked to various people in differing degrees of broken English, Spanish and Portuguese, and was helping myself to a plate of prawns and lobster, when the voice behind me spoke, with its recognizably low resonance:

'You haven't found a Bahiana for yourself, yet, Mr Tim?'

Nadia Rodriges, in a flowered backless cotton dress, smiled rather mockingly at me.

'I'm afraid not,' I said shortly.

'Is that why you were so bad-tempered yesterday? Everyone was quite frightened of you. You glowered so much and you talked to yourself.'

I managed a rueful smile, betting to myself that she knew damn well the reason for my irritation.

'No, that was not it. At my stage of life you've got over the coffee-coloured girls. Something more sophisticated is called for.'

She looked at me appraisingly. 'I do not think that you are really so sophisticated.'

'Oh no?'

'Please, do not be angry. I am reading an English book, by a man called Nevil Shute. It is about a man, an Englishman, who goes to a foreign place, and people help him because he is such a nice man. Everyone in the factory has liked you, and trusted you, in the same way. I think that you are very like that man.'

'What's the book called?'

'*Trustee from the Toolroom.*'

'Good grief. Here, in Brazil? I didn't think that old Nevil Shute novels sold here.'

'Oh yes, that one about nuclear disaster—*On the Beach*—it was very famous. I did not like it so much. I prefer this one I am reading now. I do believe that you are like this man.'

'I haven't read it, so I can't comment. I'll take it as a compliment, though.'

I was going to add that Nevil Shute had been one of my mother's favourite authors, but decided that it might be tactless. Nadia Rodriges was a few years older than I was, perhaps five or six, but it would not be gentlemanly to emphasize it.

She was still watching me from under slightly hooded eyelids. Whatever thoughts she had of me, decent fellow or retired engineer of Nevil Shute's, why spoil them?

'Would you like to dance?'

'Thank you.' She nodded gracefully.

There was an area they had set aside and some couples were quietly moving to the music. Feeling that perhaps I had been becoming somewhat truculent, I took her on to the floor and did my best, to make up. She was quite tall and her cheek came against mine quite naturally. I enjoyed dancing with her and, when the music stopped, got her a drink, finished the one I'd left and refilled my glass. She was still looking, appraisingly.

'I hope you do not mind my asking you a personal question?'

'Fire away.'

'Are you a boxer?'

I had to laugh. 'No. If I had been, I'd have had a cauliflower ear as well. No, the broken nose was a reward for playing rugby. A game for hooligans played by gentlemen.'

'The effect is very masculine.'

'Thank you, dear lady. For that you shall have another invitation to dance.'

We took to the little floor, her cheek touched mine, our bodies closed together, and thus it was that the rest of the evening went so well. A great deal of personal information was exchanged, though none of it too deep. I behaved myself, and mingled with other guests from time to time, so that it wasn't too obvious, but each time we returned to dance the closeness got closer, the grip tightened and her thigh would brush mine or press closely to me. When the party broke up and people came to leave, I accepted her offer of a lift. Mark Zuridis's cheerful farewell until Monday had an understanding smile to it.

She drove the Volkswagen through the warm night streets without speaking until we turned off the Rio Pinheiros canal and into a park, where we stopped.

'This is the University. Do you know it?' I shook my head.

'I like it here. When I am by myself I sometimes come here, in the daytime, and just sit, or walk around. I never had the opportunity to study. Now I live in a flat with my mother, who is very old, although I like her very much.'

'You never married?'

Her turn to shake the head. 'Não. I had—for a long time—a relationship with a man, an influential man, in business. Then, quite recently, I saw that he was not serious about me, that he would not marry me. I had had affairs with other men before I met him and he has another mistress now. It is over. And you, you are divorced, you have told me. There must be someone else, in England?'

'No.'

'No? Really? It would be very unusual. Particularly for a man. But you do not have to tell me, I understand.'

How did she understand? There was no understanding to do. If I tried to explain and to attempt to describe my current condition, I should simply look a fool. I had eaten and drunk well but not excessively. I was warm and relaxed, sitting in the car in the dark shadows at the side of the park. Around us, a few students walked or sat chatting and laughing around a fountain. No one paid any attention to us. I realized I was being very slow indeed. She turned to me quite naturally as I put my left arm behind her shoulders and kissed her, feeling the warm lips and moist softness of her mouth. After some time I brought my right arm down from her waist and slid my hand up the nearer thigh, under the flowered hem of her dress. She offered no resistance; her knees parted slightly wider to let me help myself.

A blaze of car headlights lit up the whole area as a taxi swept past. Nadia pulled away slightly and smiled at me as through heavy, open-mouthed respiration.

'We must stop. We are in the middle of the road.'

'I want you. Very urgently. Now.'

She shook her head. 'It is very dangerous, here in São Paulo. And elsewhere. There is much violence.'

I stared hopelessly out of the window. Everything was throbbing fit to burst. I hadn't had a woman for years, decades, centuries.

'Your hotel?'

No good. The Oropesa was the wrong place. I sat still, like a small boat waiting for a high tide to sweep it up some warm, frothy creek. She started the engine and we bumped off, back to the main highway.

'Where are we going?'

'Do not worry. The man, the businessman I told you about, there is a flat we used to use. I still have a key. He is away for the weekend, out of São Paulo. He often is. If he has not changed the lock, we will go there.'

'But what if—I mean he might—'

'Do you not want to risk it?'

'I'll risk it. Oh God, I'll risk it.'

She parked the VW outside a large old apartment building with a porticoed entrance hall. Feeling like a major criminal with unmistakable facial characteristics, I escorted her sedately across a wide lobby watched by a curious uniformed porter, who kept his face expressionless. It reminded me of an episode ten years earlier I had had with a professional tart at the reception desk of a hotel in the Rue de Douai after a Parisian rugby match.

We got in the lift, she pressed a high number, and the doors closed. I felt a little relief then, and turned to embrace her, pressing her tightly to me. My hand slid down her naked back. Her tongue darted between my lips.

Then the bloody lift stopped with a jerk, half way between two floors. She stepped back and smiled at me.

'Don't worry. The lift often does this.'

She put a hand on my shoulder, holding me while she pressed buttons and, stooping, called down the shaft through the diagonal mesh inner door to the porter below. What, I wondered, did you do when it jammed 'often' before, in here with your businessman? Did you do what I want to do now, pulling the dress away and grappling with each other, quick, against the lift walls while it bumped and swayed, gently dangling at the end of its long cable.

I started kissing down her spine while she stooped and called, sliding my hands under the dress to ease it higher towards her waist while voices answered and shouted in Portuguese, from below.

Then the lift gave another jerk, and started upwards.

She straightened and turned, smiling, to kiss me in reassurance as my breath rasped hotly from my lungs. After an interminable upward run, the lift stopped and we tumbled from the old, flapping doors. I closed everything while she went down a landing and tried a key in a door at the end. I was right behind her as the key turned and, by merciful Providence, opened the door.

She put on a dim light in the hallway.

I caught her as she stepped through a dark ante-room towards a bedroom half-lit by street lights from way down below. The flowered dress pulled off obligingly and there were only briefs beneath it on the brown warm body I scooped to my aching frame. I carried her over to the bed and rapidly, without preliminaries, she arranged herself to guide me in gasping permutations with that generous and understanding body.

12

IT WAS IN THE MORNING, when the sun came in through the venetian blinds in long white bars of light across the bed, that I remember her so vividly. I came out of the bathroom adjoining the bedroom and there she was, a great sleepy feline, striped by light and shade in rumpled sheets. I went round to her side and closed the blinds tighter to keep the sun out and she reached for me, arranging herself so that I slid easily on top of her. I took the long full upper lip gently in my teeth after our flesh had finished making its glorious uninhibited contact, and luxurious, unhurried consummation.

'You are a biter,' she said. 'Do you bite all your ladies like this?'

'Only big cats with long sensual upper lips. You smell nice.'

She moved slightly beneath me. I didn't get off, but I pulled my head back so that we could look at one another.

'You were like a thunderstorm—' her eyebrows were

slightly raised—'and very masculine. Torrential, without sophistication. Do not worry; I liked it very much. But I think, unsophisticated Englishman, that that storm has been gathering for a long time.'

'It has.'

She nodded slowly.

'Why? What is wrong? It is not good for you to—to bottle up such things. You must make love if you need it.'

'My dear sweet Brazilian Nadia, how does someone from repressed cold Northern climates start to explain such things?'

She smiled. 'I do not think you are so repressed. But I think perhaps I am not very good for you. I do not think you are very experienced with women like me.'

'What are women like you like?'

'I meant—how should I put it?—my friends say that I am someone who uses men, as she likes. I do not think so. But I have worked for two or three men, very senior businessmen, who had many mistresses, each of them, so I am used to a different life.'

'Were you their mistress, too?'

'No. Well. Only once. And as soon as I became his mistress, that man treated me badly. So I learnt.'

'It's hard to think of you as being out of control of your life, Nadia.'

'Why?'

I looked at her again. She was big-framed, with wide hips. Her breasts were not large, but the body was well-rounded and sensual. I suspected that she had enjoyed herself in some way quite independent of me, perhaps lost, during our struggling together, in some fantasy of her own. I didn't mind.

I changed the subject. 'I like your fragrance,' I said. 'Is it one of White's?'

'Não. It is called, in Portuguese, flower of orchids. Here in Brazil, you know, we can produce many perfumes. And we have all the materials necessary. Very cheaply.'

'You sound like the professional you are.'

'Thank you. I like to be good at my job.'

'However. Pleasure before business.'

'Why, what do you mean? What are you doing? Over? You like that? It excites you?'

'I like that very much. Don't you?'

'I love it. Please don't stop, whatever you do. This has been a piece of luck for me.'

And the conversation ended for a while, although I remembered it, later.

When we had slept a little more, she got up and found a robe. I knew nothing about her. She was an older, much more experienced, deeply passionate woman, Latin, of the sort that life doesn't often dish out to men like me. Whatever it was in me that attracted her, the very foreignness of me, her ideal of the Nevil Shute characters, whatever, I wasn't going to quibble with my luck. There was great strength about her; what she said her friends had deduced about the way she used men might be true. All women use men in some way and vice-versa; why should she not do so like anyone else? She obviously knew the flat well; no pang of jealousy disturbed me about that. It all seemed so natural, so true. We had needed each other badly, physically, and we had enjoyed it. The pundits of moral behaviour and the feminist proposers of unfathomable relationships would not have liked this manifestation of just plain natural appetite.

I thought of Sue, briefly, and then decided I was not doing myself any good by the thought.

Nadia was looking down at me.

'I expect you would like some coffee. You know, I am very particular about coffee, so I will make it. Would you like a cigarette?'

'No, thanks.'

'Then, please, get me one from my handbag in the other room while I put on the coffee. The handbag is on the floor where I dropped it when you were—well—you were pulling off my dress.'

She smiled at me knowingly.

I wrapped a towel round my waist and left her to fiddle in the kitchenette. The anteroom was small and I reflected that her business friend, whoever he was, had chosen the flat principally for its bedroom, not for living in. It was the classic place of assignation; no one lived in it, or could do so very conveniently. The anteroom had a sofa and a small bookshelf next to an armchair. It was gloomy with the blind drawn and I raised it to give some more light, squinting at the titles. A book on sexual technique and positions. Very appropriate. Two or three novels in Portuguese. A travel guide. A Bible. They cater for the sacred and the profane, I thought, idly. Next to the Bible, a familiar green booklet.

One of the catalogues of Sotheby's Old Bond Street art sales. Modern British Art, from the year before.

Odd. Very odd.

I opened the blind the rest of the way to let the bright blinding Sunday sun in. There wasn't much decorating the walls, either. A large photographic poster, an old advertisement for Pan American, showing a flying-boat in the air over a tropical beach with the ribbed skeleton of a Spanish galleon washed ashore beneath it. Very romantic. Another poster above an old bureau of somewhere in Rio Grande do Sul, Santa Maria, showing gauchos herding cattle.

I went over to the bureau and tried to open the fall. It was locked. There was no key.

I don't know why I did it. My knowledge of old furniture is quite practical, but I shouldn't have done it. I put my left fingertips under the top of the bureau and pulled upwards, while with my right I pushed the fall downwards. The hinges were worn and the top was flexible. The tongue of the old lock pulled clear of the socket and I opened the fall. I pulled out the lopers carefully to support the fall while it was open.

There were three drawings lying flat on the surface under the fall. They were all on rather old paper, faded with age.

The first was a sketch of a young man in a waistcoat, leaning backwards slightly as he stood, looking down. There were a few trial sketches of his shirtsleeved arms, and his head, on the same paper.

The second was of a girl in a straw hat, seated on the edge of a bed. She had an apron on. The artist had done a few sketches of her face, in profile, around the sheet.

The third was of the two together. The young man stood arrogantly looking down at the girl, leaning on a chest of drawers. She was seated on the edge of a bed, her straw hat on, apron tied, her shawl in a pool around her. In the background was a washstand with a jug on the floor. All in pencil. In the bottom corner was a faint signature: Mary Godwin, 1914.

I was looking at an original sketch for the painting I called 'A Back Room in Somers Town.'

I was still staring at it, white of face, when Nadia came in, carrying the coffee.

13

I SHUT THE LIFT DOORS with a slam, and then pulled the inner cage door across before punching the ground floor button savagely.

They're funny things, women, you know. They really are.

To think that not half an hour before she'd been gasping with pleasure beneath me and dropping tears of joy on to the pillow as I'd pleasured her on all fours.

And here I was, thrown out.

It had been bad enough when she came in with the coffee and found me, with the bureau open. She accused me angrily of prying. I thought that her white face, as white as mine, was from some fear she had, a guilt at having allowed my transgression to happen. The drawings frightened her.

But what had made it much worse was my urgent desire to know what the hell the Mary Godwin sketches were doing there. Her face set furiously and she demanded that I leave. There was a hell of a scene. She wouldn't explain. I was bewildered and angry, too. The whole damn situation was staggering.

'You've got to tell me,' I shouted at her. 'It's very important. Please! Nadia!'

Her head went back proudly and her mouth kept shut. She replied to nothing. I decided to cool down.

'I'll see you tomorrow,' I snarled in the end. 'We'll talk a lot more about this.'

'Leave! I want you to go!'

So I left. What else could I do? I dressed, made sure I had my wallet for a taxi, and entered the lift, feeling like someone caught in a vast web that he didn't understand.

The lift went down a floor and a half and jammed.

'Bloody hell!'

I pressed the button again. Nothing happened. I shouted down the shaft. Silence. I could see, through the panes of the outer lift doors, that I was stuck just about half way between floors but still high up. My gaze was almost at floor level to the landing outside. A pair of sandalled feet beneath drill trousers walked past, almost opposite my eyes.

'Ayudo! Socorro!' What the hell was Portuguese for help?

The feet disappeared. They walked quietly away. I slammed on the lift wall. I pressed the emergency button. Nothing happened.

Funny, I thought. I've seen those sandals before somewhere. Recently. And the drill trousers. On someone on the plane last weekend. On the British Council intellectual. With the black eye.

'Hey!'

I hammered on the side of the lift again. Nothing.

'Hey! *Em bas! Attendente! Sereno!*'

Where the blazes was the porter downstairs? And the flats? Did no one live in them?

Probably all fucking love nests for fornication, I thought bitterly, no wonder no one's answering. Place is a non-respondents' paradise, Brazilian style. Rotten pun, that was.

The lift trembled slightly and shuddered. The light, a central bulb in the roof, went out. Someone was mucking about with the electrics.

It was very dark. Electrically powered lifts have electrical safety devices. They depend on electricity. They also have fail-safe mechanisms, mechanical locks, clutches, grabs. Christ, they must have, I thought desperately. Unless someone has mucked them about first. The lift shuddered again and trembled; vibrations were coming down the main cables. Someone was mucking about with the winding gear in the roof. I had a sudden horrid memory of some friends of mine who lived in Madrid telling me how the lift in their block fell the length of the shaft one night, just like a stone. There was nobody in it, so we laughed.

Then the lift dropped.

It started slowly, then it started to run free, then, with a jerk, it stopped, knocking me off my feet. The vibrations increased, as though someone were trying to free a blockage. I screamed.

The window-panes were level with a concrete wall. I was trapped between floors. Looking down, I saw a gap of light, a line about eighteen inches high, in the gloom— the join at the top of the doors on the next floor down.

I pulled on the inner cage door hasp. Normally, it

locks automatically once the lift is not at a floor, so that you can't open it between floors. It opened easily.

It shouldn't do that.

There were no safety mechanisms working. None. Just me in the lift on the end of a cable, swaying gently, poised. I kicked the top of the outer doors, or, at least, the top eighteen inches of them sticking above the floor of the lift. They didn't move. The lift trembled once more and hovered.

I stepped back across the lift and took a flying kick at the top of the doors, where I could see the top safety-switch locks. They burst open, leaving an eighteen-inch gap between the top of the doorway and the lift floor, right across. I hurled myself through it hard, dropping over the lift floor edge so fast that I went right across the narrow landing and hit my head on the opposite wall, seeing stars between me and the yawning gap of the shaft below the lift.

Then the lift floor moved downwards, slowly at first, so that for a moment I thought someone was controlling it, but then faster as the whole lift, cage, roof, pulley and all, dropped out of sight. I had a vision of the free cables, whipping and shrieking in the wind of the shaft as the lift accelerated down to its terminal velocity before, with tremendous, sickening impact, it hit the basement floor.

The whole building jumped and shook as though an earthquake had hit it. Chunks of plaster rained down from the landing ceiling, covering me with dust and particles as I lay, shivering, on the floor.

The cables stopped lashing in the shaft. There was a great hissing silence.

For about ten or twenty seconds, nothing happened.

I was still sitting, dazed, propped against the wall of the landing. Dust filled the air. Through the open doors to the lift shaft I could see the grimy walls, cracked and dirty, that boxed in the dreadful space down which I had been about to plummet. I was still ten floors up.

Then life erupted.

It was like kicking an ant heap. People rushed from doors in states of dress and half-undress. I was surprised to find that there were children. Shouts and yells came from some; stunned silence from others. A woman looked at me and then at the open doors. She screamed a warning to a child and snatched it up. I got to my feet and dusted myself down. Voices boomed up and down the building. The stairway was full of people rushing downstairs. It would be a nine-day wonder. I went upstairs, mad with rage.

That bastard had to be up there, somewhere. Even on shaky legs and feeling still half-sick with fear, I knew I could pulverize the little bugger. With murder in my heart I took the stairs two at a time, pushing past people who came down in dribs and drabs from the upper floors. The building wasn't going to fall down and I was going to throw him off it when I got my hands on him.

'Tim! Tim!'

Four floors up, in her flowered dress, Nadia rushed at me as I came off the stairs. She nearly knocked me to the ground as she clasped me, embracing me with every-thing she'd got.

'Thank God! Thank God!'

I wasn't sure if it was relief at being safe herself, now that the dust was settling, or concern for me. Gratifyingly, she went on: 'You're all right! Thank God! I thought you had been killed! What on earth happened? Are you hurt?'

I disentangled myself from her and made some soothing noises. 'How far up is the roof'?'

'Only two more floors. But why?'

'Wait here.' I was a bit short.

'Tim!'

It took me only a few seconds. I found the door out on to the flat roof. There was no one in sight. The lift motor-room was boxed in a sort of shed nearby. I stepped carefully across to it and hurled its wooden door open.

Nobody. The bastard had gone.

I'm not an expert on lift gear. It looked reasonably intact—drums and pulleys and electric motors and things. But there were steel cables half-wound slackly round the pulleys in a way I knew to be wrong. A main switchboard connector was in the off position. It was no accident.

I looked outside again, across the roofs of the other suburban blocks around the building. No sign of him.

'Tim! Tim!'

Nadia's voice, echoing from the stairs, drew me back. She was distraught. As I came back down she grabbed my arm and pulled me back, to the landing and into the little apartment. I sat down heavily. I had grazed my knuckles, torn a small tear in my trousers and was still carrying dust in every crease. She babbled away at me, I don't remember what, until I interrupted her.

'A drink. Is there a drink in here?'

She disappeared into the kitchen and then reappeared, with brandy. I drank it.

'Get the bottle.'

She got it. It was a Brazilian brand. I drank a lot

more of it. From downstairs, I could vaguely hear the noise of the crowd buzzing at the base of the shaft. But for a bit of brute force they would have been extracting the remains of Simpson, T, from it. I stared at Nadia.

'Who is he?'

She gaped. 'Who is who? Thank God, Tim, I'm sorry, I'm so sorry, if after I'd sent you out you'd been killed, I would never have—'

'Cut it out. Who is he?'

'I—I don't know what you're talking about. Who?'

'The bastard in the sandals with the grey beard. He was on the plane. The same plane as me.'

'As you?'

'Yes, me. And Luis. You know? Luis White. Funny coincidence, isn't it?'

'Tim, what are you talking about? Are you all right? Please don't drink any more of that. You've had a shock. It is not good for you.'

'Your bloody friends aren't good for me either. Are they? That thin grey bugger just tried to kill me. I think he's tried before in London.'

'Oh no, Tim, you are shocked. The lift, it—it must be an accident.'

She was really very upset. The brandy was starting to work. Her eyes, luminous, wide brown eyes, glistening with emotion, looked straight into mine. There was nothing faked about her agitation. I could swear to it.

Looking round, I saw that she had closed the fall of the bureau as far as she could, but the tongue of the lock, still sticking out, stopped it from fitting back into place. I put down the brandy bottle and walked over to the bureau, jerking open the fall. The three drawings were still there and I looked down at them for a while, letting the brandy work and thinking of the painting on the easel and Motcomb Street, dead Willie Morton, Sue, and the woman at the Lord Somers tavern who'd kindly given me brandy, too. I began to calm down.

Nadia sat quite still, staring at me.

'You don't have a key?'

She shook her head, dumbly.

'Then watch.'

I put my left finger under the top and pulled upwards. I pushed my right hand down on the fall, with its old hinges, and eased it back into place until the tongue clicked back into the lock. Then I took out my handkerchief and wiped my dusty fingerprints off. Then I picked up the brandy, poured another stiff one, and sat down.

'Now then, Nadia. No one has opened the bureau. No one has seen inside. Only you and me. Right?'

She didn't nod or anything. Just sat, waiting. 'This flat belongs to Luis White, doesn't it?' No answer.

'Your businessman friend. That you had an affair with. Who owns this flat. It is Luis White, isn't, or all right, wasn't it? For God's sake, answer me. I'm not prying into your private life, I'm not going to blackmail anyone, I'm just trying to find out why certain things happen to me when that—those—pictures turn up.'

She shuffled her feet.

'All right, let's take it in stages. Luis White?'

She nodded. A miserable look came into her face. 'I told you it is all over. Tim, you do not believe that I would lie about that?'

'No. I mean I believe you.' I didn't, but still.

'So—so I—I was upset when you opened the bureau. It was irrational, I know. I just didn't want you to find out that my—my association was with Luis.'

'Very understandable. Just as I would wish to keep it from White's that I had got involved with an important secretary in the firm within which I am supposed to be doing an objective assessment. Consultants are not expected to seduce the staff. Or vice-versa. In this case, especially, in view of the extra involvement with Luis. Or ex-involvement with Luis, if you prefer.'

She looked hurt, but I had to go on.

'All that, however, is less important. Nadia, I have to know. Those drawings—do they belong to Luis?'

'Yes. Of course.' She was defensive.

'Do you know what they are?'

She shrugged.

'Não. They were always his. Or his family's. I think.'

'Were they always here?'

Clumsy, I thought, you've reminded her how many times she must have been here, up in that lift, with Luis hot for her.

'Não. I think they were not here until recently. I don't know. I may be wrong but I think they came from his house in Curitiba. But I have never been there.'

'Did you ever meet, did he ever have with him, a slightly-built, grey-haired man, British, with a tweed jacket and sandals? Might have had a beard?'

She shook her head. 'Never. Tim, what is this? I do not like it. You are acting very strangely, cruelly to me. The lift—it was an accident—such things happen here, it is not London, you know, the lift was always faulty. You remember, last night?'

Like hell, I thought. I remember last night. But that was no accident, this morning.

Her face shone at me, with innocent anxiety. If she was the lure to a trap, I felt somehow she didn't know it.

'OK. An accident.' I put down my glass. 'I'm going to wash, then we'd better go.'

I went into the bathroom and cleaned myself up. Whatever was going on, I wasn't going to get much further by pressing Nadia. When I came out she was waiting in the tidied bedroom, made up and ready to go. Her face softened when she saw me, and started to moisten.

'Tim, oh Tim, I was so frightened. I really thought you had been killed. It was terrible.'

I felt lousy. The brandy had been very strong.

'Look,' I said, giving her a light kiss, 'don't worry about it now—it didn't happen and it's all right.'

I put an arm round her. She kissed me in return. My hand was on her bare back. The kiss strengthened as she opened her mouth and pushed her tongue forward. Holding each other tightly, we sat down together on the edge of the bed.

The flowered dress came off, once again. Quite easily.

14

Dᴜʀɪɴɢ ᴛʜᴇ ᴛᴡᴏ ᴏʀ ᴛʜʀᴇᴇ days that followed I moved very cautiously, staying out of lifts and doing a great deal of thinking. I set the people at the factory a programme of market research analysis and let them get on with it. I needed time.

It had been the third occasion on which someone had tried to kill me and I was still uncertain who. Each time there seemed to be a connection with the painting, although no one apart from Nadia would know that I had seen the drawings. I believed passionately that the painting was behind it somewhere. For a while I considered whether Nadia and Zuridis were involved and that some suspicions I had about the factory were the cause of the lift episode. I ruled that out. Nadia and I might have left in the lift together; what would have happened then? What action would the plan have dictated?

What plan? Whose plan?

The Sickert and the Godwin I'd seen at Willie Morton's must have been bent in some way. Stolen or faked. From whom? Why? Willie had found something out and it had killed him. Perhaps I had some piece of information, a vital clue, without knowing it. Whatever it was, it had a connection with the Mary Godwin and Luis White. That I now knew. Nadia had told me.

'The drawings were important to Luis,' she agreed over a lunch in the factory canteen. 'A kind of—what do you call it?—mascot, talisman, something. He wanted no one to see them or handle them.'

'How long do you think he had them?'

She shook her head. 'I don't know. Tim, why is it so important? What is it about?'

I calmed her. We had agreed that during the week I would be busy and she wanted to attend to her mother in the evening at her own flat. I was unwilling to try to use the Oropesa for our meetings and I agreed that, at the weekend, we would go away together to the seaside at Guaruja, where she said a friend would lend her an apartment. There was no way I was going back to the scene of the crashed lift and the likelihood of meeting Luis, perhaps with his new lady friend.

I did need to get back my strength a little bit, too, I must confess.

I slept very well the first night or two, despite keeping alert when travelling. I double-locked the hotel room security door-latch and lay down on the bed, thinking.

Luis White was involved; the British Council man, obviously a homicidal maniac, was involved; Zuridis might be involved. I was a sitting duck, caught between the factory, the hotel and White's offices in Santo Amaro. The more I knew, the more I was in danger, perhaps, too, I was endangering Nadia and—Sue? I had a vision of Sue and myself in Willie Morton's after the attack, with Willie lying sprawled dead behind his desk, under the bookshelves full of reference books and auction records. It was a vivid memory.

There was the still life by James Bolivar Manson— why did they call him a South American name like Bolivar, I wondered?—and the sketch of two naked girls by Gus John and the empty easels. The full shelves. The reference books and auction records that Willie affected to despise, carefully arranged along the wall, where he could get at them by leaning backwards from his desk, tipping his chair.

How bloody dense I'd been. It hit me like a shock wave. There is a three hours' time difference between São Paulo and London. I had to wait till I was in Mark Zuridis's office, next morning, when he was out and I had the phone to myself. Brazil is on automatic dialling; the number at the Tate Gallery was in my little book of records I always carry with me.

It caused something of a flutter when I said I was calling from Brazil. There was panic at the other end before Sue's voice, a bit breathless, came through.

The line, for once, was clear.

'Tim? Where are you? I had to run, I was in the lower galleries.'

Her voice distracted me. I had a mental image of the slim figure, the slightly tweedy clothes and the amused, cool eyes. She sounded reproachful.

'Why didn't you ring me? You promised to call when I got back. I've been in London for nearly ten days. I thought perhaps—'

'Sue, I'm in Brazil. I had to come out here for Jeremy.'

'Incredible! Are you having a nice time?'

'Not really. How was the skiing?'

There was a silence. I hate telephones. Hate them. The scope for misunderstanding, wrong emphasis, sheer bloody buggeration of relationships is outstanding on the telephone. But her voice was soft when it answered.

'It was all right. But the weather wasn't all that suitable. They were a good party, but, look, when am I going to see you? I—I missed you.'

I flushed with pleasure, like a schoolboy. 'Probably next week. Sue, I need your help. Before I get back. It's about the Willie Morton business.'

'Oh, Tim! Do you have to? I'd almost forgotten all about it.'

'I'm sorry. Really I am. And I'm going to get back as soon as I can. But it's the Mary Godwin. I've seen the sketches for it here. The drawings, I mean.'

'Tim, are you all right? Is it very hot?'

She clearly thought I'd got sunstroke. It took several very expensive minutes before I'd given, in broad detail, a very edited version of what had happened and what I wanted her to do. Even then, I had to repeat myself.

'All of them?' she asked incredulously.

'All of them. They're listed under artists. You'll probably have to go back as far as nineteen-sixty-odd, but not earlier. It can't be earlier than that.'

'All right,' she agreed. 'For you, I'll do it. I'll want a really swish lunch, you know.'

'You'll get it.'

'Tim?'

'Yes.'

'Take care of yourself. Promise?'

'I promise.'

I must have put the phone down and been sitting there, oblivious of everything, before I heard the rather ironical clearing of a throat. Nadia was looking down at me.

'Business in England?'

And she left, with a knowing smile, before I could overcome my embarrassment and confusion enough to reply.

15

'BRAZIL,' I SAID, WITH LEADEN WIT, 'is an alcoholic's paradise.'

The men in the boardroom smiled obligingly, but without enthusiasm. It was Friday afternoon. James White, Peter Lewis, Thorburn, and Mark Zuridis sat round the table looking at me as I delivered my final peroration. The facts were simple: the Brazilian market did not have the pyramidical price-volume relationship that developed countries have. The market had a small, refined, high-price top end and a vast, cheap bottom end, in which colognes were sold in recycled litre-size wine bottles. There was only a small market between. Mark Zuridis's firm kept launching medium-priced brands for middle class millions who didn't exist yet. It was South America all over; either you have a lot of money and are on top or, like most, very little of it and are at the bottom. The middle market was very small.

So that, I had explained, was why sales were no

good. No market, no volume. Lots of stock returns. Lots of losses on stock returns. And I looked Mark Zuridis straight in the eye. He knew. He knew, that is, that I knew and that I knew, now, that he knew that I knew. It was, I explained, the only area in which I had a measure of criticism to offer. The prices for the stock returns, the old, written-down stock, might be checked before the goods were sold out to street market discounters. I measured my words very carefully.

'I believe it is possible,' I said, 'that some of the loss incurred to date might have been reduced if a more careful eye had been kept on opportunities to dispose of remaindered stock at higher prices. Such prices ought to be possible.'

Zuridis looked very uncomfortable and defended himself by talking about the poor condition that the returned stock came back in. Thorburn smiled to himself and started polishing his half-moons. When he replaced them, he flashed me a glance over the top, the sort of glance one professional gives another when they are dealing on opposite sides but understand each other perfectly.

But Luis and Peter Lewis were more interested in the market.

'You mean,' said Lewis, 'that we have to decide whether to move up-market or down?'

I nodded.

'Not that you have much choice. To move up-market you will have to license one of the famous international low-volume brands with a classy image and pay royalties. You want a volume business you control yourselves and you want to avoid paying royalties overseas, because the Government don't like it.'

That was when I made my remark about alcoholics. Brazil is swimming in alcohol, from sugar production and elsewhere. It's why they've gone in for gasohol fuel for their cars. Colognes and aftershaves and other toiletries use alcohol. There was the basis of an export business, not just with Europe and North America; Eastern bloc countries place large contracts to import toiletries and cosmetics. Brazil has the range of climate necessary to produce its own fragrances. Everything you need, in fact, for a successful local industry with a high export potential.

'High export potential,' I repeated looking at Luis and thinking, There now, you've got what you wanted, what you've been aiming for all along.

'That means import licence credits,' said Thorburn, nodding over his glasses, 'like we have in the timber business. Very useful.'

'And not only that,' I said, 'because of the range of prices for toiletries, it's impossible to establish fixed international price trends as you do in timber; trends the Government can check. If you have a subsidiary or suitable arrangement in Europe, or wherever you base your sales, you can make your profit where you want to by fixing your transfer prices. To some extent.'

I didn't have to lecture them about transfer pricing; they knew all that.

James looked at Luis. 'Cunning devil,' he said.

Luis smiled smoothly. He opened his mouth to make some sort of deprecatory reply but the telephone on the polished boardroom table interrupted him. He looked at me with the receiver to his ear. 'There's an urgent call for you from England,' he said. 'They tried at the factory apparently, who told them you were here.'

Funny thing, really. Sue would have been put through to Nadia. I wondered what their exchange of conversation might have been.

Luis sprang to his feet. 'Take it in the back office. I'll show you the way.'

He took me down a short passage after I had apologized to James, who merely nodded. A small office with a desk, chair and telephone was available. Luis had the call put through. The line was bad. Great sea monsters groaned along the submarine cable, scraping and howling and crackling at the bottom deep of the green ocean.

Well, it would have been them, if it weren't all done by satellite now.

'Hello? Sue?'

The voice was distant, anxious. 'Tim? At last. These calls must cost a fortune.'

'I'll pay. Make it quick, then.'

'I found it. At Christie's. Forty pounds. Have you got that?'

'Nineteen-sixty-four. Christie's. Forty quid.'

'Right. How are you? When will you be back? And who was that woman at the factory?'

'Why?'

'She sounded so—proprietorial.'

I laughed. 'I'll be back early next week. I'll ring you as soon as I land. All right?'

'All right. And Tim, do be careful.'

'I will. 'Bye Sue.'

''Bye.'

Click. Silence.

Outside the office window I could see distant hills across hot dusty buildings and shimmering roads. People in light-coloured flimsy clothes sauntered or hurried alongside the rowdy traffic. Big clouds moved across the sky, making the sun duck in and out of light and dark, but keeping everyone hot, loose; muscles relaxed. Much flesh was bared. The London I had just put the phone down on would be coming to the end of a cold February Friday afternoon; people huddled in coats and hats would be splashing the bitter damp pavements towards the trains that would carry them through the flashing lights of dark suburbs to an evening inside, watching the telly and blocking out the draughts. No one would be thinking of the mass exodus tomorrow to the beaches of Santos and Guaruja, the ice-creams, hot dogs and baking sand. In England, it would be the telly, bad news and irritable Saturday shopping.

A tale of two cities. Perhaps of two women.

You can get very bored sitting on a beach, I thought, going back to the boardroom. A life of applied hedonism and plentiful sexual opportunity would be all right for a while, but then you'd need something more serious in your life, something to achieve, creation of some sort. Culture.

Codswallop. There's a lot of damned dull stuff in Proust, isn't there, Mr Mortimer? Books are a load of crap, Mr Larkin; I know that.

Luis White joined me in the corridor. Why wasn't he back in the boardroom? Listening in somewhere, I thought, stiffening. What did he know? My mind had wandered right off Mark Zuridis's business, because events were beginning to fit together and I was preoccupied as we re-entered the boardroom together. I had to refocus my thinking with a jerk when Thorburn said:

'What comes next?'

They were looking at me, expectantly.

'You have to make some decisions. It's over to you now. I've put everything I've told you into some notes in the three-page memo I've given you all. I'm obliged to Mark's secretary for typing it all up so promptly.'

I looked at Luis as I said that, thinking of Nadia, but he avoided my eye, so I went on:

'I'm not writing a report, because there's no need. No one'll read it, anyway. You know what's up and I guess Luis and Mark will take it from here.'

I started folding up my papers. I was feeling impatient. I thought I knew, now, why Willie Morton had been murdered and I wanted to get on. Tiredness and tension contributed to it. Hard work and the chance of being killed were not exactly relaxants.

James White and Peter Lewis showed some consternation.

'But is that all? Aren't you going to stay to develop some strategies for the products and so on?'

'No. I'd be wasting my time and White's. Once you've decided your basic strategy I'm sure Mark and his team will be far better at identifying what products are best for Brazil, not me. I've just been an observer and I have a business to get back to.'

Thorburn cut off any further objections.

'I agree with Tim. I'm sure we're grateful to him for carrying out what has been a first-rate audit of the situation. From now on it's up to the local team. I've no doubt Luis will want to get down to it with Mark. Especially the export potential, for which he is more than adequately qualified.'

His grin was not lost on anyone. 'It has worked out extremely well all round.'

He leant across to shake hands with me. 'I'm sure we'll meet again, Tim,' he said. 'How long are you staying here?'

I hesitated.

'Are you staying for the Carnival?' Luis put the question languidly. 'I'm sure you deserve it.'

'Er, no. I'm going back early next week. I'm staying the weekend with, er, friends.'

'What, here in São Paulo?' Thorburn inquired.

'No. At the coast. Guaruja.'

'Quite right too. Enjoy yourself.'

He nodded to me and moved off. James and Peter Lewis shook hands. I accepted a lift with Zuridis, who offered to drop me off at my hotel. He suggested that we meet up with Luis at the factory on Monday, before I left, and I agreed. Luis insisted on accompanying us to the car and said farewell, shaking hands with me as though Monday were a long way off.

I know. I should have gone straight back to London, but there was business to clear up in Brazil and, well, yes, a weekend with Nadia in prospect.

All right, Mr Clever Dick, as Willie used to say; what would you have done?

16

THE ROAD FROM SÃO PAULO to Santos goes out past the Volkswagen works in a long red dusty highway until it brings you down off the edge of a 3000-foot escarpment to the coast. They have built a spectacular highway to do it but, back in 1867, a British surveyor called Daniel Fox and a load of railway engineers built the Santos-São Paulo-Jundiai Railway which climbed 2,600 feet up the Serra do Mar from Santos in four inclines over a seven-mile stretch. At the time, it was said to be the steepest incline of any railway in the world. Until that railway was built, São Paulo was a sleepy town of 25,000 inhabitants, but the railway opened up the coffee trade to the coast and transformed the city, turning it into what it has become.

All that is gone now. Railways are old-fashioned and Brazilians hate anything old-fashioned. They reconstructed the gradients around 1974 and made it a rack railway with new electric locos from Japan.

My father told my mother that back in '38 he was talking to one of the British railway directors in São Paulo and the man invited him to dinner.

'Evening dress,' he said. 'Black tie, old man.'

My father pointed out that he was a working engineer, not a St James's Street clubman, quite apart from the weather. They had no air-conditioning, then. He didn't travel with evening dress in his case.

'Oh dear,' said the director. 'What a pity. Next time, perhaps?'

All that is gone, too, thank heaven. Nadia made me drive her Beetle. She was happy. She watched me as I braked and changed gear, weaving the little pig of a car in and out of the traffic.

'You are a good driver,' she said. 'I think I could fall in love with you. It excites me.'

'In England,' I said, pompously, 'the ability to drive competently is not considered sufficient excuse for a girl to give a man her all.'

She giggled and put a hand on my knee. I was keeping an eye on the rear-view mirror to watch the crowded straggle of cars following us. The sun shone and my shirtsleeves billowed in the breeze caused by the speed and open windows. Nadia wore a light backless top and a striped pleated skirt split at the waist where a cord tied it. Her bathing costume was underneath.

When the sea came into view she cried out in pleasure, gazing out of the windows as we wove down the steep edges of the hills on the descending road. Before Santos, the Piassaguera highway forks off to the coast for Guaruja and into small wooded hills with dense subtropical vegetation. Inland there are lagoons; up the coast northwards there are beaches of every sort, private and public. Europe has nothing like it.

We drove through the town centre, looking a bit like Benidorm without the fish and chips, and out a little way northwards. No one was following us. Nadia directed me to turn off the coast road, up an inland avenue to a low block of flats. We parked the car in a service area behind, under a straw-roofed port to keep the sun off. We went round to the front of the building, up an outside stairway to a balcony running along the front of the first floor. There were three flats; ours was the end one.

Holiday week-end places are the same in any hot climate. Living-room, bedroom, kitchenette with a service stairway to the back, bathroom. All with cold, tiled floors. One rug in the sitting-room. Chairs with wooden arms, a table and four single chairs, settee. A double bed and built-in wardrobe. Basic stuff. There were a few decorations, prints and a tourist poster of São Luis do Maranhão, showing the old colonial town on the island. It was nearly midday and getting hot outside. Nadia unloaded some provisions, gave me a Coke to drink and went into the bathroom. I took a look outside, leaning on the balcony rail. A few people in bathing gear sauntered down towards the sea. Cars shimmered in the sun. It reminded me of a holiday Carol and I had once taken in Spain. I went back inside.

I was looking at the poster of São Luis, thinking of the contentious Cochrane and his two ships anchored off the island in the steaming equatorial heat, having fooled two Portuguese armies, when Nadia came out of the bathroom. She smiled and I took her in my arms, standing up, and kissed her. The top she wore above the pleated peasant skirt was backless and my hand felt the firm bare flesh around the strong spine. Her mouth opened and her kiss grew moister. The back of a woman has always excited me. As I investigated further, the split skirt opened at the side and the rounded bare flesh of more exciting regions came into my hand.

'Hey,' I said. 'You had your bathing costume on underneath this before. It's gone. Don't you want to swim?'

She put her head back, still holding me, and looked into my face from under hooded eyelids and downswept lashes.

'Não,' she said. 'I don't want to swim. Not now. That's why I took it off.'

She made it all so easy.

Later, after a siesta and some refreshment, we went in the car to a beach in the late afternoon sun and swam lazily. No one followed us there, either. Watching Nadia bathe, that strong, almost stocky body plunging confidently, I thought of cool Sue Westerman and grey London streets, wondering what Sue's slender frame would look like if you took off the careful clothes she wore.

In the evening we went to a restaurant, sitting outside under the bright warm stars, drinking Brazilian white wine produced by Italian immigrants and eating delicious fish stew. Music somewhere played sambas and folk songs, Candomble rhythms from black African-originated cultures mixed with Catholic religion. African negro slaves were imported for the sugar plantations until the British stopped it, forcing the Brazilian government to a showdown between 1845 and 1850. Bless the

Royal Navy; I felt sentimental and warm, chatting quietly but distractedly with Nadia until she too, in her way, forced a showdown.

'Disco or back to flat?' she demanded.

'Discos are for any time. Let's go back. Can we drive up somewhere with a view first, for romance's sake, then go to bed? I need you badly.'

She laughed and led the way to the car.

We drove around some unpaved tracks she knew, up hills until, suddenly, the trees opened out and we were in a clearing above the sea. The water glittered way below, with occasional lights until, southwards, a brighter shine came from Guaruja itself. We sat for a while taking it in and I put my arm around her shoulders. I had the unworthy thought that, like the lift and the flat, she'd brought people here before.

'This is beautiful,' I said. 'Life doesn't often deal the cards this way. You must be my lucky angel.'

'That's nice. That's the first time you have been really nice to me, d'you know that? You are very masculine; very potent, sexually, but a woman really likes to be romantic. I know you think it's silly, practical Englishman, but for us it is important. I liked you from the start. Now I like you, very much.'

She kissed me, arousing other instincts, but her sense of responsibility and danger refused further progress in the car. We drove back to the flat and were quickly in bed, raising each other to heights I hadn't climbed before, on in the darkness for a long, long time until, eventually, fondly and in friendship, we kissed goodnight and fell asleep. I was drained and sated, lying under a sheet like some male animal of a pack who has served the females in his charge repeatedly and lies, with normal aggression spent, content within his lair. Nadia slept beside me. I had a strange released emotion before I nodded off, a feeling of total detachment and escape, 3000 miles from all my responsibilities.

It was the scraping of the kitchen door as it opened, just a quiet grating noise of sand on gravel under the bottom edge, that woke me.

Nadia slumbered deeply. I slid out of bed and put on a pair of shorts I had left lying on the floor. My limbs were still relaxed and heavy. Past the bedroom door, half open, I could see a little way into the living-room but not much. Moving cautiously on bare feet, I slid through the door quietly and into the centre of the tiled living-room floor just as, with blinding strength, the light snapped on.

He was standing framed in the kitchen doorway, gun in hand, light on his feet, grey-haired but the beard shaved off. The man from the British Council. I malign the British Council; murder is not one of the folk arts they promote. He had a grey sweatshirt, grey slacks and light running shoes on. The gun was a smallish one; I blinked several times in the light before I could come to believe that it was real. I hadn't reckoned on a gun; he hadn't used one till then. Damn fool, I thought, of myself.

I'm not an expert on guns, but I didn't move. The funny thing was that, now that we were face to face, so to speak, I wasn't frightened of him at all. He was too slight to be taken seriously, yet I knew he was like a snake, quick and deadly, more athletic than I was. He raised the gun slightly, like a man getting ready to aim, pointing it accurately. I noticed him stiffening, as you do when you are about to shoot, when Nadia appeared, naked, at the bedroom doorway. Her sleepy voice interrupted him.

'Tim, what are you doing?'

It was said in a drowsy tone, curiously, as though she was mildly surprised by my absence from her attractive side.

Then she saw him.

'Oh, Dios, oh não, Tim—por favor—'

'Shut up!'

The voice snapped. He was rattled.

"One peep out of you, lady, and you're finished. Get back in that bedroom.'

Scotsman. Glasgow. Unmistakable accent. Now that I could see him closer, I noticed the flushed colour of his face, the broken veins, the signs of whisky and short temper. He gestured at me with the gun. I stepped back a pace. Repeating his warning, he stepped across to Nadia, who covered herself with her arms as best she could.

'In the bedroom. Get back on the bed, face down. One noise and you're finished. Do as I say and you won't get hurt.'

Like hell, I thought. He'll finish me here and then you'll be at his mercy. He'll enjoy himself with you before he does you in, too. It would take a real cold-blooded professional to resist a helpless naked woman with a body like Nadia's. Especially begging for her life.

Her face was frozen with terror. All those warnings about muggers and their attacks on courting couples suddenly come home to roost. We had locked the doors as a precaution, yet here he was, inside.

He gave her a push and she stumbled backwards. He took the key from inside the door, moving into the room with her but keeping the gun on me. For a moment they were in the room together, he fully dressed, she lying naked, faced down on the bed. I had a flash of Sickert-vision, seeing the tension and horror of the view with eyes that pricked until I realized I must blink to clear them. Then, with a meaning grin, he locked the door and came towards me.

'Bad luck, Simpson,' he leered. 'Been enjoying yoursel', haven't ye? She's no' a bad bird, eh? Bit old, mebbe. You should be grateful to me. I could've done ye in earlier just now, but I thought I'd let ye have one last fling. Not that you deserve it: you've been a bloody nuisance.'

Why don't you scream, Nadia, I thought desperately, like Sue did, for Christ's sake, why don't you? Like so many victims, do you really think that if you do what he says he'll spare you? Why don't I scream, come to that? Save your breath; it's too late for that now.

'Like killing birds, do you, Jock?' I managed to make my voice full of calm scorn. 'Where d'you learn that? Clyde-side? Like the winding-gear, eh?'

An irritable frown crossed his face. 'Winding-gear? What winding-gear?'

'The lift, MacTavish, the lift. Where d'you learn about lifting gear, eh? Cammell Laird? Or G. and J. Weir perhaps. How to release lift safety mechanisms. Not very good at it, were you?'

His face creased into a scowl. It was my only hope. There were only seconds to go.

'Call yourself an engineer, perhaps. Not you. What

were you? Welder? Miner? Eh? Not up to much with your hands, anyway, are you? Had to get yourself a gun, did you? Brave boy. No bloody good with a knife, were you?'

It was working. He was angry. He took a step nearer, gun poised.

'Ah'm an artist, Mr Fucking Simpson—expairt, that's what I am. Not like you. I'm a real artist, see? A painter.'

'What of? Ships? Plimsoll Lines? What would you know about painting?'

He was livid. 'Ah wairked on the Clyde, but I went to night school. Glasgow School of Art. I worked like a dog. For what? Made bloody redundant by bastards like you. I know more about painting than you'll ever know, technique, drawing, etching, the lot. I can turn out a painting that you'll never understand or detect, you sod.'

'You should have stuck to welding, Jock.'

'Welding? Welding? What fucking use was that? Eh? All I got from welding was to be thrown on the scrapheap, Mr Fucking Efficiency Expert, by a bunch of sods like you. That's when I started painting full time. I'm a bloody good artist, I tell you. Came South. Deprived of a decent living by Sassenach bastards.'

'Balls. Rubbish. Decent living? You idle bunch of drunken sods. You never did a stroke, any of you. Clyde Shipbuilders. Come in to work in the morning and lie around. Didn't even have to make ships. Just sit there and let the stupid English taxpayer pay you for doing sweet FA.'

'What? What?'

His face was suffused, scarlet. He stuck his

inflamed countenance out at me. Just what I wanted. You should never do it.

Never do that to a left prop forward who's spent his youth in provincial pubs on Saturday night after the rugger match. Never. Especially when what you are anticipating is hand or arm movements.

I snapped my head forward with the force of neck muscles still strong from years of ox-like grinding in muddy scrums. They call it putting the nut in. It doesn't hurt you at all if you know what part of your skull to use. And the opponent's nose is so soft, so tender, full of blood and sinew, gristle, with little bone.

The impact smashed his.

His head reared back first, then fell forward as I recoiled and his hands came up instinctively to clasp the splattered, blood-spurting mess, numb with shock and pain, the mouth gaping open to scoop for breath that wouldn't enter the splintered nasal passages.

I grabbed the gun with my left hand as it came up and used my right to give him a front-row forward's short hook to the entrails. Up and under. His whole body jerked. He gave a sort of wet grunt and sticky fluid spattered my face.

Still holding the gun, I stepped back and used the right to hit again, this time the wheeling overarm chop to the side of the neck that I'd tried on him in the playground at Somers Town and half-missed in the dark. I didn't miss this time. I thought of Willie Morton, the knife and the lift. I put everything I'd got into it.

His head snapped sideways and he went over backwards, leaving the gun in my hand. His feet shot out from him as the rug skidded underneath. He hit the tiled floor with a great wet smack and his head snapped back the other way as it hit the wall close to the floor, leaving him flat out with his head at an angle cramped into the skirting.

He lay dead still. Literally.

Once there was a bloke in a rugger match I played in at a Northampton tournament, broke his neck in a flying tackle. It was awful. They took him off on a stretcher but he died later that day. I remember the sickening crack in the tackle and the way he looked lying in the wet grass. Wing three-quarter, he was.

The intruder didn't have that long. He was dead, then and there. I'd hit him too hard. That and the way he fell. I knew immediately I looked at him, inert as he was, on the floor. I felt ill.

'It was him or me,' I said, half out loud, to reassure myself. 'Honestly, it was. Him or me.'

Putting the gun on the table, I unlocked the bedroom door. Nadia was lying shivering, face down on the bed.

'It's all right,' I said. 'It's me, Tim. It's all right.'

She gave a sort of cry and buried her face in the pillow. Then her arms went tightly round me, not for love, but for her own reassurance. After a while I pried her loose and got us both a very stiff drink. The shivering eventually ceased and I got her a robe. I haven't had to cope with women in shock very often but I remembered something my mother had said about keeping people warm.

It took two stiff ones before I had the courage to search the body. His name was Lomax. He had his passport and a driving licence with him. Born Glasgow 1940. Older than I was. A set of keys for a rental car. Some money, more keys, odds and ends. In his side pocket there was a piece of paper with a printed letterhead: 133 Clarendon Street, London, NW1. Scrawled on it was a brief list:

Simpson—Guaruja.
The girl
Tate Gallery
Monday.

I put it in my pocket.

Grey light was coming in the windows. Soon a glorious dawn would be breaking, sunlight coming in from over the sea to the east. Sunday morning with families who slept in late, eventually headed for the beach. Happiness everywhere.

I emptied his pockets.

She came into the room as I put all the things I had taken on to the table.

'When will you call the police?' she asked. 'Shall I?' It was a remarkable calmness she had. Her face was still white but she looked at me, relying on me completely for guidance. I'd told her he was dead while comforting her in the bedroom.

'No.'

'Wh-what? Why not?'

'Because I'm not going to spend hours and weeks explaining to the Brazilian police what all this is about; how I've killed an intruder who also happens to be British in very suspicious circumstances. He's not an ordinary mugger or intruder, is he?'

'I—I don't know.'

'Don't you? Well, he isn't.'

'But still—you should call the police.'

'And get Luis into it as well?'

'Luis? What do you mean?'

I was shaky. There was unpleasant action to be taken. I snapped. 'I mean Luis! Your Luis! Yes; your Luis, still. This man worked for him. They followed me together to Brazil. Luis took the Congonhas route and this Lomax took the Viracopos. That way they covered me. You said your affair with Luis was over months ago. Well, I doubt it. One of the photographs of a promotion on Zuridis's wall is quite recent. You are in it, Zuridis and Luis. It was you that told him about Zuridis, wasn't it?'

Her mouth trembled. 'I don't understand you, Tim, what is wrong? Are you jealous of Luis?'

'No, I'm bloody not. You're welcome to Luis. The sooner I get out of here, the better. I'm not letting Lomax's body stop me, either. But you told Luis about Zuridis. You told him that the books were being fiddled. The obsolete stock. He sold the remaindered stock to market traders at a huge discount. They must have put backhanders in cash into his pocket in return. It's an old story. I've checked the street markets—he's way out of line. He agreed the stock write-down figures in the books and pocketed the difference. You must have known—you're too bright not to. And you are Luis's— friend. You told him.'

She straightened up. Her face darkened.

'Oh, come on, Nadia, it was pillow talk, wasn't it? You thought that he might marry you.'

She said nothing, but her eyes answered.

'It was Luis's big break. He blackmailed Zuridis into supporting his presence as a director. Odd, it seemed, because he'd always opposed the perfume company before. Until he was told—it was your idea—about alcohol and perfume exports. Just like you told me. There's an old saying about a consultant being a man who borrows your watch to tell you the time. You did it beautifully that night in São Paulo. In fact he probably prompted you, he or Zuridis. One or the other—or both—they laid you on for me. Didn't they?'

Her face congealed. Became a mask, with deep hollow eyes and rigid mouth, half open.

'The mistake they made was the drawings. In Luis's flat. What a blunder. Or didn't Luis think you'd take me there? Not to his love-nest. Zuridis put me in the Oropesa. Not renowned for encouraging lady friends, is it? So I'd rely on you for suggestions and you'd take me somewhere known. Like you did here. Somewhere where our friend here had the key—the key Luis gave him. I could be at his mercy like I was in the lift.'

Tears were beginning to flow down her face, soundlessly, in an awful stream. She began to shake her head from side to side, her whole body swaying.

'Stop! Stop! This is horrible! What do you think I am?'

'In love with Luis.'

She stepped back to a chair and sat down heavily.

'It is true, isn't it? He's never married, for—for emotional, superstitious reasons. But he's quite normal. Isn't he?'

She nodded. Her voice was broken. 'You make it sound awful. It wasn't like that. I did want to help Luis.

I told him about Mark; you are clever to guess at that. And I told him how he could use the company for exports—he was so frustrated, so tense; it was an obsession with him to get some money put away outside Brazil. Anywhere. But particularly England. I don't know why. It was the family, I think. He wanted to be equal to them in their own territory. I wanted to help him. But he and Mark, they didn't—they wouldn't dare—suggest that I did what you are saying. Just to put the idea in your head that's all. So that the suggestion would come from you, not them. An independent source. It wasn't so difficult, was it? Not such an original idea.'

I felt a rueful pang. Nothing original, she meant, not from me. All I had been was a useful stud and stool pigeon.

She took my hand. 'Tim, believe me, I liked you. And I was angry with Luis, he neglected me so and he—he seemed more interested in how I could help his business than me. As a woman, I mean. You needed help. Please don't say I was just like a—a prostitute, like that. Please.'

She was crying again.

'I've never seen this man. Never. It is horrible. Like a nightmare. I thought he would kill you. And then kill me after he'd—he'd—' She shuddered.

I felt like a prize shit. It seemed to me that Luis had a real piece of Latin womanhood to cope with in Nadia. This bloody maniac of a Scotsman would probably have done us both in as she said. She wasn't a party to his crimes. Just to helping Luis in his career in Brazil. That had nothing to do with Somers Town; I saw that now.

I was a prize shit. A prize shit in a dead panic. The grey filtered light was beginning to creep across the room giving everything a ghostly look. I squeezed her hand and then took myself away.

'Luis will have to explain this to you. I'd be asking some nasty questions if I were you. Very nasty questions.'

She stared at me. 'What do you mean?'

'Later. It's getting light. Put a top and trousers on and bring your Beetle to the back kitchen steps. Quick.'

'What? What are you going to do?'

'Do as I say!'

I must have frightened her, because she did it. Truth to tell, I must have looked pretty desperate. To have your mild Trustee from the Toolroom turn into a lethal pugilist must be fairly terrifying, too.

I pulled Lomax away from the wall. It took a good deal to pick him up and sling him over my shoulder. I took him down the back steps and slung him into the back of the Beetle, on the floor, out of sight. Nobody saw us.

Sometimes in the early hours, when the horrors prowl, I still have the screaming habdabs thinking of that inert floppy body with the dangling legs and arms that wouldn't go into the car the way I wanted. I had to heave him around and pull the head and shoulders from the other side so that the legs could be folded in and the doors shut. Whenever you want things to fit in a hurry they never will. It's called the innate hostility of inanimate objects. Or something like that.

I made Nadia direct me to our lovers lookout point of the previous evening. It was getting lighter all the time. Day comes quickly in hot countries. A few times, on the main road, I had a vision of being stopped by the police on a routine check and could see the newspaper headlines: POLICE STOP COUPLE WITH BODY IN CAR! Once we turned off up the dirt road, I felt better. We wound up through the trees in the early light, seeing tropical birds calling cheerfully to the new day. Nadia still shivered uncontrollably from time to time with shock.

In the daylight the clearing seemed smaller, which pleased me because it meant we were less on view. I stopped the Volkswagen near the edge and got out. A beautiful sunrise was coming up over the sea, dispelling the morning mists. Birds and crickets sang and cheeped. Out to sea, but far out, boats were moving to fishing grounds. There was no one else. The drop was not very sheer, but enough to give a reasonably clear fall to the rocks below. Nadia sat with her eyes tight shut. I pulled Lomax out by the shoulders and heaved him to the edge, getting him in a lying position parallel with the face. I thought hard of Willie Morton and the attempts on my life, then I rolled him over.

There was a sort of scrabbling flutter, a rushing of pebbles and a sloppy flailing thump or two. Silence for an awful few seconds, then a heavier thud, very distant.

Exit Lomax.

'Funny, Nadia,' I said, 'how we seem to have this thing about places we occupy before we go to make love in your flats. They recur in the morning with unpleasant consequences. First there was the lift in São Paulo and now the lover's leap here. Funny, eh?'

It was a pretty nasty thing to say, but I wasn't feeling very good.

She burst into tears.

I drove carefully back to the flat, scanning the roadside as we got nearer. The hire car was another Beetle, parked two hundred yards from our door. I checked the number on the label with the keys. At the flat I cleared up the blood that Lomax's nose had splashed on the floor and the wall. Then I cleaned everything carefully, including the doorknobs. One of the keys from his pocket fitted the back door. Nadia tidied the bedroom, packed up our things and cleaned herself up. She looked at me with dry eyes now. Neither of us spoke. I made her drive to Lomax's car, then I took his and drove it carefully to the middle of Guaraja, leaving it in a public carpark with the keys inside. Then I got in beside Nadia.

'To São Paulo,' I ordered.

She put her hand on my arm. 'Please,' she pleaded. 'I am too upset. Drive me back. Let me have this one pleasure before you—you leave me. Please.'

So I took the wheel and it was while I was driving speechlessly back on the long highway that I thought about that list in Lomax's pocket. Simpson—Guaruja. That was me, all right, due for the chop. Well, Lomax was the one who got chopped.

The girl. That was Nadia. Or was it? He hadn't written Simpson and the girl—Guaruja. Just Simpson. The girl was written separately. And there had been many times when he could have picked Nadia off, quite easily, alone. It suddenly hit me that he had never been after Nadia, never, because almost certainly Luis wouldn't let him. Why write 'the girl' separately?

Tate Gallery. Monday. The only address they knew for Sue was the Tate Gallery.

Sue was the girl. Her phone call to me had been intercepted by Luis at the board meeting.

And so it was that, at Congonhas, where everything was shut because it was Sunday and British Caledonian didn't have a flight to London so I booked Varig, I eventually dug up someone who was kind enough to check the outgoing British Caledonian passenger list, first class, to London the night before.

Luis White had gone to London. Ahead of me.

When I left Nadia she kissed me passionately, and wept. 'Please do not think badly of me. I am a little in love with you and you have been a wonderful lover to me. Please write to me. Promise me?'

'I promise.'

'Oh, thank you, Tim. I will wait for your letter. I want to stay your friend. I cannot help it about Luis. You do see that? I love him, you see that?'

'Of course.' I felt like a piece of wood. Wormeaten wood.

And then, kindly, she said: 'Tim, you do not mind if I give you a piece of advice?'

'No, of course not.' I was barely listening to her.

'It is a stupid life, this travelling you have done. You must choose one place and stay there.'

'Thanks. I'll remember that.'

And I left her, crying after me as though I really mattered to that passionate, instinctive woman. The plane took off, and, eventually, as we left Rio and the lights of Brazil receded into the darkness, tears stung my eyes. But the voice of the friendly Varig man obsessed me, needling me the whole night long.

'Why yes, sir. Mr Luis White caught the British flight to London last night. He will be there already, this morning, Sunday.'

In good time to be at the Tate Gallery when it opened on Monday morning.

17

I GOT TO THE TATE GALLERY around ten-thirty. The flight had been late into Heathrow and there was no reply from Sue's flat. Fuming with impatience, I tubed in to Earl's Court and caught a taxi to Millbank. It was very cold.

The pillar-porticoed terraces of Earl's Court and Chelsea, in varying degrees of smartness and seedy nonentity, reminded me of Camden Town in the white, winter morning light. Scruffy London streets of grimy grey brick, cleaner now, incredibly, than they would have been sixty years ago. It was almost a relief when the taxi debouched out on to the embankment and swept past Vauxhall Bridge to drop me off outside the gallery.

She wasn't there.

They rang down from reception in the echoing hall of the Tate to the administrative offices below. No luck. Then one of the women at the desk remembered.

'There was a gentleman called for her earlier,' she said helpfully. 'Asked for her specially. Said a Mr

Simpson—is that you?—had sent him. She went out with him. I noticed. He looked so sunburnt, lucky man.'

She smiled at me triumphantly, happy in the knowledge that I'd made a monumental cock-up of something. I took the steps outside the Tate in flying jumps down to the roadway and leapt into a taxi.

'Clarendon Street,' I shouted to the cabbie.

'Which one, sir?' he countered, quick as a flash.

I made a guess. 'Somers Town area. North of Euston, somewhere.'

He nodded and ground off in low gear. 'I know where Somers Town is, guy. Let's see, Clarendon Street. Runs parallel with Eversholt Street, don't it? Think so, anyway. Lots of Clarendon Roads, there are, but only two or three streets.'

'Probably. Yes, I think so.'

Thank God, I thought, I'm in the hands of a professional. 'Which end, guv?'

'A hundred and thirty-three. Please hurry.'

'Oh. Emergency, is it?'

'Yes.' Dear God, how much more?

'Hunnerd and Firty-Three. Up towards the Oakley Square end, I think it is, innit?'

Oakley Square. Mary Godwin, 68, Oakley Square, 1914. There had to be something innit.

'Yes! Please hurry. Please.'

'If money's no object, guv, I won't go acrawse to Piccadilly. Take me own wye, longer like, but a bit quicker, orl right wiv yer?'

'Yes. You choose. The quickest way, whatever.'

'Oh, good. Gets a bit boring, guv, regular work. I likes a bit of a challenge.'

I had a sudden surge of emotion. My eyes stung again. I was glad to be back, anxious, but glad. In the hands of a homegrown cabbie, bless him, honest, well-intentioned man. He moved at speed all right, in and out of cabbies' runs through back streets, hitting the Marylebone Road, then Euston Road, then, oh relief, Eversholt Street down the side of Euston Station and round, not far from the Lord Somers, into Clarendon Street. Razed to the ground at the south end. Two old terraces left at the north end, either side of the road, leading up to the blocked-off back of Oakley Square. We were on the west side of Somers Town.

One hundred and thirty-three was a pillar-porticoed terrace house of cheap eighteen-thirties construction in not bad condition. Two flats. I paid off the cabbie, tipping heavily.

'Orl right for you, guv? Ta very much.'

'Damn good. You were fast. Credit to your profession.'

He grinned. More pleasure lit up his face than the tip had done. 'You're a gent, guv. Good luck to yer!'

I may need it, I thought grimly, as he ground off.

Two doorbells. One for the lower basement, no name on the tab. One upper, with a fading inked name against it. Lomax. I pushed the front door cautiously. It opened. There was no one on the ground floor. I went through up the stairs two at a time, first floor, no one in the front room so I charged through to the back.

It was a light room, facing north-east, rather empty except for an easel and a chair or two. Sue was sitting in one with her head turned towards me, surprise on her face.

'Tim! Thank heaven!'

Standing over her, almost menacingly, was Luis. His hand was rammed into his jacket pocket, making an ominous but somehow not very convincing bulge. All round the room, ranged along the walls for viewing, like a gallery, some of them hung, some simply propped along the skirting, were the paintings. They were all there. About twenty of them.

There was the Sickert I had seen in Willie Morton's, with the woman still sprawled openly on the bed and the man sitting, in his waistcoat, despairingly beside her. There was another, where you could only see the top half of the woman, nude, because the man was in the foreground, sitting slightly more upright but wearing his jacket this time. Two more Sickerts, interior studies of nudes in a bedroom, like the Mornington Crescent ones, with a venetian blind across the window and a toilet mirror on the chest, obscuring the light. Next to them were two Ginners that looked like 'Flask Walk,' but he painted 'Flask Walk' after 1918, I thought, so they must have been somewhere else, and two Dieppe scenes, one a wet street. Interiors by Gilman, one of a room with flowered wallpaper a bit like Mary Godwin's, probably Maple Street, and a café with a woman sitting at a table with a cup on it. There were several studies by Augustus John, mainly drawings, one recognizably Ida, his first wife, and another obviously Dorelia, his second. Probably done at the same time, when they were all living together. Two Bevans, both Camden Town streets, with horse and cab plodding along them; a Sylvia Gosse of a nude on a couch in a room with a big mirror and a chair. My eye turned to a view of St James's Park by Malcolm

Drummond and then three Spencer Gores, two of them views across Mornington Crescent Gardens from No. 31 showing the new red tube station and the spire of Old St Pancras Church in Oakley Square in the distance. The third was a small music hall scene in the Alhambra. Last of all I saw the Mary Godwin, with the young man looking down on the girl, separated from the others.

About three or four hundred thousand pounds' worth. Maybe more, even half a million if handled right by a clever dealer, like, say, Willie Morton. For each of them there was a drawing, a preparatory sketch or study of some kind, clearly original, sometimes two or three. They were amazing. I took them all in slowly, walking round the room while nobody spoke. I turned to Luis.

'You couldn't be satisfied, could you,' I asked him, 'with just what the drawings might have fetched? I know, it would have been a few thousand rather than hundred thousand pounds, but for Christ's sake, how much money do you need?'

His face moved for the first time, breaking the horrified stare he had given when I entered the room.

'It's not how much I need, my dear interfering Tim, it's where I need it. I need it here, not in Brazil. England has no exchange control. From here I can do what I like. From here I can send money to Switzerland, the Caymans, the States. Anywhere I like. For ever. It would be put away safely. You like Brazil. See how you would like it if you knew that your money was tied forever in a country with one hundred percent inflation and a deal of possible political instability. And see, as well, if you were tied to those Whites in Santo Amaro, with no say over here, nothing.' There was great bitterness in the cultured voice. Hatred, even.

'So you got your friend to produce all these, using the original drawings as the base, and reproducing the colours and techniques from the paintings in the Tate, and a dozen other museums. Your forger—it was Lomax, wasn't it?—was brilliant. These are all very good. Old canvases, old frames here and there, carefully composed pigments and colours. It must have taken a long time. Did you pay him a living while he worked for you?'

He nodded. The hand was still in his coat pocket. Sue stared at me and him and the paintings in turn, her mouth open in disbelief. I decided to go on.

'The drawings belonged to your grandfather. You found them in the old house at Curitiba on the coffee estate. Around nineteen-sixty-two? And then you had a shock. You were in England later, doing your time at the Bank like a good little foreign distant cousin. You took an interest in this period because of your family, your grand-father. Didn't you? British art of this period was cheap, then. And you bought a painting at auction. In nineteen-sixty-four. For forty pounds. That one.'

I stabbed my finger at the Mary Godwin. He flinched.

'It was genuine. It was the painting that she produced from the drawings in your flat. The drawings you kept sep-arately. Why? Was it after you bought the fruit of the drawings here that you had the idea to make up the rest?'

I was glaring at him. He didn't answer. The menace seemed to have gone out of him. I caught, once again, the look of vulnerability that I had seen in the lunch room at Santo Amaro and pressed on.

'I want to know, Luis. I need to know. Because that painting killed Willie Morton. And I said the words that did it. I reminded Willie of his reference books. He had auction records going way back. He was a professional. So, after I left that day, he looked up those two paintings for curiosity. Odd, wasn't it? They weren't supposed to have been in England since nineteen-fifteen. It was a tremendous coup for Willie: But he was cautious. The Sickert wasn't recorded so that was probably OK, it would be, wouldn't it? Lots of Sickerts weren't exhibited or recorded. And the Mary Godwin that just had sentimental value wasn't for sale, so it was hardly worth bothering. It was just there to lend credibility. He looked it up, as I did. Exhibited at the New English Art Club, nineteen-fourteen. Great. No problems. Then Willie did something unforeseen. He checked right back to see what Mary Godwin had been fetching at auction. And he found it. Way back in his records. Where he shouldn't have; Christie's, in nineteen-sixty-four, sold for forty quid. To you, actually.'

Luis said nothing. His eyes went over to the painting. His face had started to drain of blood under the tan and he looked ill.

'So Willie knew it was all wrong. There was a con, somewhere. From then on he would have been on the alert. I don't know how Lomax would have dried and processed the paintings but Willie would have gone over them like a terrier looking for a rat. He'd smelt one. And he tackled your friend Lomax right away. Lomax knew the rat would be out and running if he didn't shut Willie up. He was a violent bugger. He killed Willie then and there with a paper knife off the desk. He took the paintings to the van outside and came back to clear up. Then Sue and I walked in. You know the rest.'

I walked across to the Mary Godwin and turned it round.

'There it is. In faint pencil on the back. Someone noted the bidder's name on it in pencil. White. That's what Willie meant when he called my office and talked about a coincidence. He was really alerted; once he knew about its sale in the 'sixties he checked it all over. And there was the name. Your name, Luis.'

I put the painting back down again. Sue sat still, immobile. She had taken her eyes off the paintings and was watching us. Luis still stood with his hand in his jacket pocket, still facing me. I decided to end it.

'Don't pretend. You haven't got a gun. You haven't the guts to kill anyone. You're just a big soft playboy who's had life pretty easy and got out of his depth. Lomax was the killer, not you. An accessory to murder, though, you are—after the fact—and a conspirator to defraud and Lord knows what else. You moved into a nasty sticky world and you're covered in slime. What is more, you sent Lomax to kill me—twice in Brazil—and I think you were expecting him here this morning, to finish off the rest of the work. With Sue.'

I must have looked pretty menacing. He took a step back, away from her.

'Well, you've had it, Luis, because I killed Lomax last Saturday in Guaruja and now I'm here. To fix you.'

He crumpled then, sitting down heavily in a chair away from us, head bowed forward.

'I didn't! Believe me, I didn't want him to! I got to hate Lomax. I couldn't stop him. We went to São Paulo to follow you and see why you went. I didn't think he'd try to—to—'

'Get off! You knew he would! He'd killed Willie Morton and you knew that.'

'I tried to stop him going any further. But he was mad. He'd worked so long on these paintings. He was to have half of what they brought. I offered him the rest—my half—to stay in Brazil until things blew over. He was-n't to come back here, today or any other day. I got him to agree to that. He threatened me—he had too much on me. I'd willingly have paid him my half to end it all.'

'I believe that. Because, ironically, between Nadia and Zuridis and me you'd found the way to get your money out. By exporting perfumes and toiletries. Over a period of time you'd have had some money out anyway. But Lomax wasn't in on that. He wanted his lump sum. Badly. Badly enough to kill me. And Sue, just in case she'd recognize him again. He was mad all right, barking mad. And I'd found the connection with you, which he needed anyway to sell this lot. It was a brilliant idea. These drawings—you found them in your grandfather's trunks at Curitiba?'

He nodded.

'Collected together at art schools from his teachers and people who'd helped?'

'Yes.'

'But how the hell did you expect to get away with it? A collection as important as this, undiscovered? The drawings I can understand, what authenticity they'd give. But the Whites here would never wear it. I asked Jeremy before I left if there were any paintings, and he said—'

'Jeremy! The Whites!' Luis's eyes flashed. Anger

shook his voice. 'Those bastards! What would they know? What would they care until there was money in it? Eh? My grandfather's things were practically undisturbed. There could easily have been canvases there as well. Most of those Camden Town paintings are quite small, particularly without frames. They'd fit into a trunk, easily. What could the Whites say? They never bothered with us. My grandmother wanted to forget England and they put her on the estate at Curitiba, well out of the way, until she died. My father never went near the place. They brought him up in São Paulo. My mother was Brazilian and these things meant nothing to her, or to anyone else. It's only recently that this period has started to be worth any real money and then only in England. It's not an international taste, like French Impressionists and it's only a minor national offshoot of them. Paintings keep turning up all over the place. Lots of them have been lost.'

'Ideal for a fraud of this kind.'

'Fraud? A fraud is it? What about me? What about my family? You bloody superior British and your bloody superior attitude! You're a fraud! I'm as entitled to a place here as anyone! That bloody Bank and those swine in charge of it. They won't help me, give me a chance here. They forced me to go back. To the jungle as they think of it. My own family!'

There were tears of self-pity in his eyes.

'My father and my grandfather, they gave their lives for this country. Isn't that enough? Eh? What do I have to do? Bleed to death all over Buckingham Palace steps?'

'You've got a British passport. You've probably got a Brazilian one as well, knowing you. Haven't you?'

He didn't answer, but his face told me I'd probably hit some truth.

'You're damn lucky. You're entitled to residence here and there. There was nothing to stop you coming here like any other man and getting a job, was there?'

'You're wrong! Absolutely wrong! I'm not entitled to residence here any more! Like some poor Ugandan Asian, or something!'

'That means,' I said, 'you must have chosen to commit yourself to full Brazilian nationality at some stage. You've made your choice. You should stick to it.'

He put his head in his hands. 'If only I'd known! When I left Eton I never thought I'd want to be involved here again.'

Bad luck, Luis.

I walked to the window and looked down at the dirty little London garden below, at the back of the house. Not a garden to cultivate; a garden, more likely, in which to bury things, bones, old iron, scrap, dead bodies. Bounded by yellow-black brick walls and broken trellis.

'You should forget about England,' I said. 'Just as I'll have to forget about Brazil. There's no extradition treaty between Britain and Brazil. Ronald Biggs could've told you that. You've committed a crime here and I've done one there. Mine was justified, self-defence, but I'll not risk it. It will soon be all meaningless. We'll change places. The British did things that changed the history of Brazil. They built railways and altered everything economically. They changed the population by stopping the slave trade. Cochrane captured the whole of Maranhão and Pará for Dom Pedro the First and sent Portuguese armies packing. What does it all mean, now?'

He said nothing. Head in hands, he sat among the splendidly faked art around him.

'I've not got through to you, have I? What I'm trying to say is that nothing lasts for ever. And in South America it lasts even less. Cochrane got nothing for his efforts; the railways fell apart or into other hands; the British were busy with an Empire elsewhere most of the time. They couldn't expect to have South America as well. The best thing Whites of Santo Amaro can do is to become Brazilian properly. You forget England and I'll forget Brazil.'

He wrung his hands. 'That's history! It's not now! The White Bank here could help me but they've done nothing, not here. I even had to use Zuridis to lever myself back into affairs in São Paulo.'

I suddenly felt very sorry for Luis. Every choice he'd ever made had been the wrong one at the wrong time. It's not difficult to do.

'Luis, you don't understand. It's not just you, a distant, distant cousin from overseas. Their own son and nephew, Jeremy, he doesn't get a place at the Bank either, and he's not nearly as distant as you. The English can be very unfeeling about relatives, especially junior relatives. As for the superiority thing, I don't go too much for that. I've often said that if you want to find a real, old-fashioned, superior Englishman you have to go abroad, because there aren't many practising ones left here. This is a socialist democracy. Your relatives at the Bank and in Santo Amaro are dinosaurs, like old Indian Army men, superb but redundant.'

I came back from the window. My mind was made up.

'Stop feeling sorry for yourself. You've never had a hard life. Did you expect to be given a job for ever? Your short cut to riches—where did you find Lomax, by the way?'

'Around the rooms. He was an artist. I used to go regularly but I paid him to watch for me when I couldn't make it, just to see if—if there'd be another—'

'Another what?'

'Sight of them.'

'Who?'

He pointed at the Mary Godwin. His face was congested with emotion. 'My grandfather. My grandmother. There, in the picture. There they are. In nineteen-fourteen. They were destitute. My grandfather was still trying at art, abandoned by the family.'

'The family in Brazil, you mean. His father.'

'All right. Maybe. But the English family too, and they knew how hard life here would be without money. So they had to do some modelling; after all, it was my grandmother's profession. Artists were kind to them. They let them have a few sketches from time to time. This one they did for Mary Godwin in a room not far from her lodgings for a few shillings, anything to bring in some money.'

My mouth opened. That was it. Why the man looked superior to the girl. He was a White. She was a model, the one he married. The painting was very perceptive.

'They modelled for her in their own bedroom. Not far from the Hampstead Road. I found the drawings on the top of the second trunk I opened, in the early 'sixties, before I came back to England. The Swinging Sixties.

There was a note of my grandmother's with it. She modelled for Mary Godwin and Sylvia Gosse and she moved to Chelsea with the baby in nineteen-fifteen to be nearer Mary Godwin, and other artists there. I watched all the Mary Godwins coming up for auction in the 'sixties. There weren't many of them. I nearly had heart failure when this came up. I'd have bid anything for it. You see, by then I'd found this address and, when it came free, I took a lease on it. I was crazy to trace anything of the family here. It was in my grandmother's notebook, in early nineteen-fourteen. "Clive and I modelled for M.G. in the bedroom at 133 Clarendon St." This is it, Simpson. We are in it. The back room in Somers Town.'

There was another silence. None of us moved. All three pairs of eyes looked at the slight painting against the skirting. Away from the Sickert, on its own, it still had a sad quality. There was less of the dramatic tension of the master it emulated, more pathos; not the grand melodrama, but the secondary emotions of the daily struggle for existence. In a year, the young man painted there would be dead, in France or Belgium, gone with countless others. The girl would end up in Curitiba. My eyes turned away from the canvas, taking in the window, the mantelpiece, the place where the chest of drawers he had leant up against had stood, and the walls. The paper on them was all wrong now, and the atmosphere had totally changed. How could they have known, in early 1914, what their fate would be? That nearly seventy years later their grandson would sit here and weep for them with two strangers? What a ghastly mistake. The one genuine painting in the whole lot, put in temporarily as a minor work to lend credibility, had blown the whole grand deception apart, killing two men. Just because the dealers and investment men, people like Willie and me, wanted price records.

'There's just one more thing I have to know,' I said to Luis. 'Why did you bring Sue here if what you say about Lomax staying in Brazil is true? To this haunted house of yours? This is where Lomax worked, isn't it? I came near that night in December and he thought I was getting too close. He attacked me. But you—you haven't it in you to do that to Sue. What did you bring her here for?'

He looked sheepish. 'I thought I'd bring her here to see if—to see if she'd—the paintings—'

'To see if she'd think they were genuine?'

I was incredulous. He nodded dumbly.

'Sue, did you think, that they really were—?'

She nodded, just as dumbly. Then she spoke. 'It was the drawings. The studies, sketches for the actual paintings. It made everything so convincing. That man must have been a near-genius.'

'He couldn't sell his own work,' Luis said. 'No market for it. He was too versatile, almost. Galleries wanted something consistent, nearly always the same. Once an artist does something popular, that's what he has to stick to. Russell Flint with bare Spanish bosoms. Conan Doyle with Sherlock Holmes. Lomax hated it. He could paint anything. Perhaps that was his trouble.'

'That and homicide,' I agreed, sarcastically.

Luis looked up at me, quite passive. 'What happens now?' he asked.

Decision time.

I walked across the room and collected up all the drawings. I put the Mary Godwin painting on top of them, then I carried the pile across to Luis and dumped them on his lap.

'In this country,' I said, 'you might get a sentence of up to five or maybe even ten years. I'm told the average time a life sentence for murder lasts is seven years now, and I guess you might serve four. It was Lomax who was the murderer and he's dead. You're weak. I don't know how much would stick on you, anyway. It would have to be proved, all of it, including intent and all that.

'My advice to you is to go back to Brazil. You and Zuridis will make a fine pair of running mates. You can cheat each other blue, but watch out for that Scots accountant, Thorburn, I'm telling you. For God's sake, take your drawings and go. Sell the lease on this place. It's unhealthy. Camden Council will probably knock it down soon, anyway. I'm letting you go partly for Nadia, who for some reason wants you badly. I don't expect you'll marry her because the Third World War will break out if you do. But only partly. The real reason is for what's owed; two good men in line whom you've never seen and who didn't get much of a break here. Let's say that we've balanced up the score; we owed you and now we don't. You're in luck with me, Luis.'

He looked up at me, partly in hope and partly in fear.

'The paintings? What about them?'

I looked at them, ranged along the walls. The murderous Lomax's legacy of lights and darks, colours and subfuscs. What was it called? Chiaroscuro.

'Sue and I are going to put them under our arms and take them into the garden. We're going to burn them. All of them.'

And that is what we did.

He watched us, motionless, from the bedroom window. As the flames got higher, I remembered a story of Somerset Maugham's about South America, called 'The Man with the Scar,' in which a political prisoner about to be shot was allowed one last wish. He kissed his adored wife goodbye and, while doing so, knifed her to death so that she would not be left, sorrowing, behind.

The officer in charge of the firing squad then let him go.

I think Luis White felt rather like that man.

18

I WASHED AND SHOWERED, feeling drained. Sue made coffee in my grubby little kitchen. She walked carefully round the room I occupied in the Fulham Road, looking at this and that. It was mid-afternoon and the light was starting to go, but I had gas heating and the place had warmed up fairly quickly.

When I washed, some sunburnt skin flaked off my forehead and she smiled faintly at the sight.

Burning the paintings had given her a tremendous emotional shock, like seeing the *Hindenburg* in flames in New York or watching the *Titanic* go down. Her face was flushed and hot. Her eyes were dilated like they are on someone who has been at the cinema for several hours and then comes out into the sunshine. When she had finished her coffee she put it down carefully and we sat looking at each other over my stained coffee table.

'You let him go,' she said simply.

It was a statement. Matter of fact, with no questioning in it, not really needing an answer. But I did answer.

'Yes.'

She looked expectant then, so I went on. 'They don't hang murderers any more. And accomplices get even less.'

She smiled. 'But don't you think—'

'Yes, I do. But he'll go. He won't stay. And there is another point.'

As though on cue, my telephone rang. I answered it in front of her. It was Jeremy.

'Tim? My dear fellow. Tremendous news. I had no idea you were back already. I've just spoken to Sir Richard. He's frightfully pleased. Some man he relies on in Brazil called Thorburn has rung him up and said that it has all gone very well. My uncle regards Thorburn as the only professional in the place, apparently, dotes on his every word, keeps the whole thing together. Canny Scotsman type, you must have met him? Well anyway, he says that you did a frightfully good job and didn't miss a trick. My uncle's really very pleased. Feathers in caps all round. Look here, are you all right, why didn't you stay for Carnival?'

Admirable, excellent Jeremy, of course I was all right. I made a few soothing noises.

'Should have stayed, Tim, do you good. Look here, they're all very chuffed that you found a place for old Blanco—my cousin Luis, I mean—keep him occupied, what, out of mischief, eh? Important to the family, that. Really can't say how pleased everyone is, you never know, now, what it might lead to by way of closer ties with the Bank. Why not?'

And on he went, genial, benevolent, money-making Jeremy, loving to be liked, loving to dish out praise, largesse, happiness, like a small boy throwing chocolates to his friends.

'Well, take your time, Tim, getting back I mean, must be exhausted after that frightful long flight. Hate flights myself. Must dash, Tim, Geoffrey wants to review some figures, very tedious, sends his best—what—oh, yes, asks how the dusky maidens were? Really? Never! Talk it all over when you come in. New ideas for the investment fund—absolute winners—very well, Geoffrey—must go—'

Click.

She still sat waiting as I put down the phone.

'You see,' I explained, 'I am my master's loyal servant. Keep it in the family. What good would it do to haul Luis to the police station, cause a sensation, all in the papers, member of venerable banking family in art fraud murder scandal shock horror probe. Not very good for my career, that.'

Her face didn't register disapproval, as I had expected it to. Not at all. But her eyes, softening, slightly, looked through my screen.

'Don't rationalize it all now, Tim, with nasty self-seeking commercial reasons. And don't pretend to be the humble family servant either, even if it does you a bit of good. That wasn't the reason was it?'

'Wasn't it?'

'No. I was watching you. You really meant it, didn't you, about wiping the slate clean? For his father and grandfather. There was something else too. I think it had to do with your own father. I saw it in your face. You'll have to watch that sense of history of yours, Tim, or it will hold you down like a ball and chain.'

'Look who's talking. I'll try to watch it, if you want me to. I rather thought it was a sense of fair play.'

She smiled and looked down at her hands. 'Can I use your bathroom? I'm still dirty from the fire.'

I took her through the bedroom to the bathroom which led off it, thanking heaven that it was reasonably clean. She closed the door and I wandered round, taking things out of my case and hanging them back where they belonged. When Sue came out she sat on the edge of the bed and watched me.

'What will you do now?'

I was a bit surprised. 'Go back to Park Lane in a day or so. Who knows, Jeremy seems to think that my rating is high with the Bank, I might do more for them. Become one of their young whizz kids.'

'I think you'd be making a mistake. Stay with Jeremy.'

That surprised me, when I thought of what she'd said before about art investment funds and advisers. I stopped unpacking and leant up against the chest of drawers to look at her.

'Why do you say that?'

'I don't think the role of a company ferret would be good for you.'

I had a vision of Nadia's tear-stained face at Congonhas, telling me to stop travelling.

'Why?'

'I don't think it really suits you. I think you need to stabilize your life. You obviously have a very retentive memory and a strong visual sense. It's ideal for an art investment specialist. There are thousands of ferrets, Tim, all ferreting away for other people, but very few art investment specialists. You should try to stay different.'

I looked down at her. It sounded like good advice. She had taken off her jacket and was sitting in her white blouse and neat plaid skirt. She looked very clean and refreshing. Then she spoke, again.

'I'm sure I'm right.'

'Yes, but I've still got a pretty limited knowledge, you know. Of art, I mean, especially earlier art. I'm concentrated on a narrow period here and there.'

She smiled. 'I could help you. I think you have two problems, Tim. One is about mutual interests and the other is, well, let's say you have a rather Latin and masculine view of sexual relationships. The first I know I can help you with. The second, well, I can't promise anything, can I, of course, but I could try. After all, I am— well—I—' Her voice trailed off.

I was standing in my shirtsleeves looking down at Sue in her blouse as she sat on the edge of the bed in a back room in a house in Fulham Road. I had a startling realization of the scene we were enacting. I was also being very slow.

Crossing to the bed, I broke the tableau we had made and sat beside her. She turned to me and we kissed, slowly at first, then with more intensity as I helped her to unbutton the blouse.

Well all right, Mr Clever Dick. What would you have done?

If you enjoyed
A Back Room in Somers Town
by John Malcolm
we hope you'll like
the following opening chapter of
Landscape of Lies,
another art-mystery from
Felony & Mayhem Press

1

‘Y OU MAY BE RICHER than you think, Michael. Come over here and I'll show you why.’

Julius Samuels smiled and lifted a glass to his lips. The liver spots danced on his old throat as he swallowed his whisky. It was not quite 10 AM. He was seated in a worn mahogany swivel chair and wearing a white coat smudged with paint. His left hand held a large oval-shaped palette with squibs of pigment laid out in a curved spectrum near the edge. A cigar thicker than a thumb burned in a tray on a shelf near his right shoulder.

Michael Whiting picked his way past stacks of gilded frames, tins of oil, bottles of varnish brown as beer, rows of canvases, their faces turned confidentially to the wall. He edged around a large easel, careful not to snag his corduroy suit on the wood, and stood next to the massive bulk of London's most venerable picture restorer. Behind and below them the traffic in Dover Street rumbled forward in the sunshine.

In front of the two men, on the easel, stood a painting. It showed a woman: her skin was pale but she had the faint blossom of pink in her cheeks. She was wearing a blue hood—except that half the hood was missing. It had been removed by the restorer. Under it was revealed a thick mane of chestnut hair.

Samuels reached for his cigar and drew on it. The end glowed like the curly filament in a small lamp. 'I took off the varnish, then applied some diluted acetone and white spirit.' He cleared his throat. 'The blue came off straight away, as easy as wiping your nose. I found all this lovely hair underneath. Then I found the earring...that's when I called you.' He wedged the cigar back into his mouth.

Michael was examining the chestnut hair. It was beautifully painted; he could almost count the strands. 'Perbloody-fection. But why would anyone cover up such lovely hair with that hideous hood?'

'Rum bunch, these Victorians. But I've come across this before. People were more religious then than they are now. Italian religious art was fashionable in those days—and that made it expensive. But it wasn't hard to "doctor" one of the family portraits, which were much more common and therefore cheaper. Get a nice-looking woman, safely dead so she couldn't complain. Cover up the jewels, the cleavage, the fashionable hairdo. In no time you have a portrait of the Blessed Virgin.' He chuckled, though it sounded as if he was gargling. 'They were rogues in those days.'

Michael smiled, carefully keeping his eyes on the picture. 'You should know.'

Samuels replied without removing the cigar from

his mouth. 'Have a whisky, Michael. You're not thinking straight this morning. I sometimes "improve" paintings, I know. All restorers do. That's what customers want—old masters that look as though they were painted at the weekend. But—I never invent.' He reached across for the Bell's and a glass.

He continued as Michael helped himself. 'The reason I phoned you was this: if you give me the go-ahead and I clean all this Victorian mush away, you might be able to identify the lady from her jewels. There might even be a coat of arms in the background. If you can identify her you know better than I do how much that will improve the value of the picture. That's why you may be richer than you think.'

Michael's eyes were watering slightly from the strength of the whisky so early in the day but he tried not to let it show. He felt a quickening of the pulse that wasn't due to the alcohol and stared again at the canvas. This was one of the main reasons he had become an art dealer: for the thrill of discovery. True, he loved just looking at paintings. English ones especially. Michael thought English painting was very underrated across the world. The Americans appreciated it, but the Italians, the French and the Germans had never regarded English art as equal to their own. The few occasions when Michael had sold paintings to foreign museums had been the proudest moments of his career. But the discoveries he had made—those were the most exciting times.

He leaned forward to inspect the picture again. The hair and the jewel were certainly a cut above the blue hood. As old Jules said, underneath this dreary Victorian saint, which he had acquired at a house sale along with something else he valued more highly, there might just lurk a much better painting.

Julius had taken down from a shelf a large book. Like all good restorers he kept a meticulous record of what he did to paintings. He made notes and little drawings, partly to cover himself should there ever be any dispute about the authenticity of something he had restored, partly as an *aide-mémoire* in case, as regularly happened, a work came back to him on a later occasion. He opened the book and showed Michael a tiny drawing on one of the pages. 'This is how much I've taken off so far. The rest shouldn't take me too long. What do you think?'

In reply, Michael placed his hand on the old man's shoulder. 'If this woman turns out to be Lady Luck, Jules, it's not going to do your liver much good.' They had a deal that Michael always paid in whisky, to avoid the tax man.

Samuels gave a throaty chuckle. 'Michael, by my age your liver becomes your favourite and most useful organ.' Samuels chuckled again and the liver spots did another jig on his throat. He pointed at Michael's glass. 'Knock that back and let me get on. You must have a shop to go to.'

This time Michael laughed and finished his drink. Samuels delighted in calling dealer's galleries their 'shops': he knew how it hurt their sensibilities.

Out in the sunshine, Michael turned south, towards Piccadilly. He had broken his cardinal rule of never drinking anything other than single malt whisky—as he always did when he visited Julius. But he was smiling; an encounter with the old man always put him in a good mood.

He dodged the traffic in Piccadilly and walked down St James's Street. He passed White's, turned into Jermyn Street, then right opposite Fortnum and Mason into Duke Street. His own gallery was in Mason's Yard, half-way down the street on the left, through an archway. It wasn't Duke Street itself, of course, or Old Bond Street, come to that, but it wasn't bad. He and his partner could afford more space there, and anyone who knew anything about British painting knew where to find them.

He passed a couple of other galleries. In the window of one was a portrait and he stopped to admire it. It was a small Degas pastel, smudges of powdery pink, pale blue and apricot splashing out from the dark charcoal lines. It showed a middle-aged man, bearded and balding, but elegant in a close-fitting jacket and a high collar, with a flowered handkerchief cascading from his breast pocket. A comfortably off figure from the comfortable world of the nineteenth century, the world of servants, bicycles, picnics. A world that lots of people wanted to return to, in art if they couldn't do it in real life.

Michael looked past the portrait to his own reflection in the window. Corduroy suits, he had been told a thousand times, were a thing of the past. They reeked of jazz and coffee bars, the archeology of the twentieth century, in the words of his ungovernable younger sister, Robyn. But, at thirty-three, he couldn't quite bring himself to abandon what he had got used to. Nor was the art dealer's uniform—dark, double-breasted suit, sea island cotton shirt, black shoes, shiny as olives—all that enticing either. The brown velvet of the corduroy suited Michael's colouring too. He had been even blonder as a baby but he was still very fair. Robyn was jealous of his hair and its waviness, even though he couldn't seem to keep it in place. His gaze shifted to the cigar in his hand. The tobacco was a weakness, of course. Cigars were expensive, made him look older than he was, and lots of people, women especially, hated the smoke. But Michael was hooked. He loved the smell, the crackle of the leaves, the colour of the leaves. He relished the deliberate ritual of cutting and lighting a cigar, of rolling it in the flame of the match. He rolled the cigar between his fingers now, then jabbed it into his mouth and straightened his tie, using the reflection in the window.

Michael sighed. He always seemed to have an unravelled look, no matter how hard he tried. He took another glance at the apricot splashes in the Degas and moved on through the archway which led into Mason's Yard. His gallery was at the far end where its sign could be seen by passers-by in Duke Street. The green and gold lettering read: 'Whiting & Wood Fine Art'. Michael had a partner, Gregory Wood, an accountant who had many contacts in the City. All galleries had to borrow from the banks so that they could maintain sufficient stock to give customers a decent choice. If Greg could borrow money at a better rate than other galleries were getting, they were ahead of the game.

Michael and Greg got on well—they had to, given the fact that they were a small firm and in each other's pockets for most of the time. While Greg raised loans and chased customers who hadn't paid, it was Michael's job to find the paintings and the customers. The only slight shadow on their relationship was coming towards Michael now as he opened the door to the gallery and stepped inside. The pleasure Michael took in their current 'star'—a small Gainsborough oil sketch, a landscape with a low, pepper-coloured horizon and a firebrick sky—was soon wiped out as Patrick Wood greeted him.

Had Patrick not been Greg's son Michael would never have allowed the boy—for he was barely twenty—anywhere near the gallery. Snobbish, pompous, someone who imagined that dealing in paintings made him better than other people, he was a not unfamiliar type in the art world. Worse, a thin gold chain dangled from the buttonhole in his left lapel and he affected brightly speckled bow ties. Today's was pink with dark red spots.

'Good morning, Paddy.' Michael knew how Patrick hated being addressed as if he were an Irish bricklayer. 'What were you doing in the inner sanctum?'

The 'inner sanctum' was the viewing room at the back of the gallery, where favoured customers were shown paintings they might like to buy. It had easy chairs, a hidden bar and two velvet-covered easels. Access to the sanctum was supposed to convey a sense of privilege, or achievement, denied to ordinary mortals. Patrick had just stepped out of it, leaving the door half open.

'You have a visitor. I was hoping to keep her all to myself—though it seems she's here to see you.'

'A woman?'

'Not just any woman, Michael. This is Rita Hayworth, Princess Diana and Zelda Fitzgerald all rolled into one. As the Michelin Guide might say: "Well worth a detour".'

Michael grinned at Patrick. The boy was improving,

almost human. 'Keep that up and we'll have you writing catalogue entries soon. Think you can make some coffee without spraying speckles on that lovely bow tie?'

Patrick nodded. These sparring matches were normal and they both knew Greg approved. He said he wanted the spots knocked off his son.

Michael cast a brief glance over the walls of the gallery. It was late May and the art world was preparing for its big season, June through to mid-July. Soon Michael and Greg would be putting their best wares on the walls in readiness for the foreign collectors who would descend on London for the big auctions and the fancy antique fairs. For now, however, the gallery was showing some of its less intimidating pictures: a small Hoppner portrait, a Cozens landscape and a wonderful, almost abstract, cloud study by John Thistle in peach, cream and crimson. Michael adjusted the picture, which was not quite straight on the wall, and went through to the inner sanctum.

The room stuck out at the back of the gallery with nothing built above it, and Greg and he had been able to equip it with a glass roof or skylight so that pictures could be viewed for much of the time in natural light. The sun streamed in through the glass panels and on to the woman who was waiting. Patrick had not been entirely wrong. She wasn't young enough to be Princess Diana but she had the Hayworth hair, long and sweeping down the side of her face so that it almost covered one cheek. Deep eyes, dark as damsons. A warm, wheat-coloured skin. But the face was dominated by the sharp arch of her eyebrows, which were somehow curved and angled at the same time. It gave the woman's face an amused, quizzical, sardonic cast. Michael noticed that she had a thin plaster across one cheek. She hadn't taken off her rain-coat, hadn't even unbelted it; that, he supposed, was what gave her a Fitzgerald air. It was as if she had an open car waiting for her nearby.

'Hello,' he said, holding out his hand. 'You're here to see me? You're not the taxman, I hope?'

She stood up, smiled, and shook hands. In high heels she was an inch or so shorter than he was—taller even than Princess Diana. Her hands were surprisingly rough. 'Isobel Sadler.'

'Please sit down,' he said. 'I've just been to see a man who insisted on offering me a large Scotch—at this hour!—so I for one need some coffee. Would you like to take off your coat?'

The coat masked the woman's figure so he was disappointed when she refused. Instead, she unbelted it and let it hang loose. Underneath she was wearing a white cotton shirt and a kilt. She sat back in her chair and crossed her legs.

Before she could speak the phone rang. Michael picked up the receiver and took a fresh cigar from his top pocket. As he listened he lovingly rolled the thick tube between his fingers. 'I don't believe it,' he said into the receiver. 'Again? Imbloodypressive. How many divorces is that—four? Five! Yes, I'm in, of course. Good idea. Three weeks, I'd say. If Miss Masson is divorcing, it can only mean she's ready to get married again. Okay? 'Bye, Nick.' He replaced the receiver, licked the end of the cigar and began to fiddle with his matches. 'Sorry about that. Where were we?'

Isobel Sadler said, 'It's good of you to see me. I

gather it's normal to have an appointment. As if you were a doctor.' An eyebrow lifted a fraction. A mocking movement?

Michael shrugged and breathed blue smoke into the room. 'You're lucky I'm here,' he said. 'I travel a lot. You might have wasted your time.'

'I hope I'm not wasting yours. Edward Ryan suggested I come to you.'

'Oh yes? I wonder why.' Ryan was a dealer in oriental things. Michael tapped the first of the cigar ash into a lacquered tray.

Isobel Sadler smiled. 'He said you weren't too old or too young, that you weren't too rich or too hungry, that you weren't too straight or too bent, and that you liked a gamble.'

'Hmm. Who are Ryan's solicitors? I'll sue.'

'Save your money. He also said you thought like a detective—that's why you've made so many discoveries. Well, I have a mystery for you.'

As she said this, Isobel Sadler reached down to a packet at the side of her chair. From the shape it looked like a painting. She unwrapped the paper. Michael admired her movements but noticed once more the rough skin on her hands. In profile, her nose was too long to be perfect, and in an ideal world her lower lip would not have been so fleshy. But those eyebrows, which seemed to move independently of the rest of her face, gave her expression a jolt of electricity, radiation as much as warmth. It was one of those faces where none of the individual parts was in itself remarkable but where the whole added up to considerably more than the sum. Michael liked it.

She got up and placed the picture on one of the velvet easels, then sat down again in her chair.

Michael looked at the painting. He could usually tell straight away how good or bad something was but it was hard on people to respond too quickly. They were more flattered, and more convinced, if he took his time over it, and less devastated if the verdict was unfavourable.

He noticed immediately that the frame of the picture was broken at one corner and that some paint had chipped off nearby.

The picture showed a landscape of sorts. There was a valley in the background, and some buildings behind a copse of trees. In the foreground was a ring of figures— he counted nine—and, it appeared, all were male. Each figure was dressed differently: one was in a tunic, another in what looked like a monk's habit, and yet another appeared to be a skeleton wearing a mitre. One of the figures lay in front of a ruined window that made a kind of arch, through which the countryside could be seen. The ruin contained a number of columns, one with a carved capital, and to one side there was what looked like a small chapel area screened by a red cloth.

Conscious of Isobel Sadler's eyes on him, Michael stared at the landscape for a while, pulling on his cigar. So Edward Ryan thought he liked a gamble, did he? Gambling was just one of Michael's sins. Most of the other things he enjoyed—whisky, cigars, red meat— were rapidly becoming crimes these days. He let the smoke fill his mouth, then breathed out slowly, feeling his chest and shoulders relax: the taboo comfort of tobacco. He got up and examined the picture more closely. It was not in good condition. The panel was cracked in at least three places, and one of the cracks looked quite new. Besides the paint loss he had already noticed, there were patches of dirt and discoloured varnish. He turned the panel over. Sometimes the back of a picture told you more than the front: who had owned it, when it had been sold and where, whether its supports had been changed.

Not this time: apart from the fact that two of the cracks went all the way through to the reverse side of the panel and there were several worm holes visible, the back of the painting told him nothing new. He replaced it on the easel, sat down again and tapped more ash into the lacquered tray.

'No problems here for the taxman. Your picture has decorative value only, I'm afraid.' He wondered if Miss— Mrs?—Sadler knew that this was the time-honoured way of saying something was virtually worthless. 'It is probably English, northern European certainly, but not by anyone I recognise…Not that I am the best judge,' he added quickly. 'Although it says "English paintings" on our window outside and on our business cards, our speciality is really the late eighteenth and early nineteenth centuries. Your picture, I would say, is much earlier—sixteenth century by the looks of it, and to judge from the panel…However, apart from the poor condition it's in'— Michael pointed with his cigar to the cracks and the abrasions—'it is a very odd composition. To put it bluntly, it's not at all well painted.' He tapped one of the faces, on the right of the picture. 'This head, curiously, is well done, but the rest'—he waved his hand over the other figures—'are very weak, clumsy even. The proportions are wrong; the heads are awkward on the bodies and the features on some of the faces are coarse.' He said all this as gently as he could, not wanting to crush his visitor's hopes too harshly but at the same time not wanting to mislead her. 'I must say I have never seen such a composition before.' He pointed to the figure in the tunic, which had curly designs on it. 'This man, who appears to be holding a clock, looks like some sort of mythological figure.' He pointed to another man. 'This one seems to have a sort of plant growing out of his middle—I haven't a clue what that is. Very odd.'

He stared at the picture for a while without speaking, then turned to look at Isobel Sadler. Her hair had fallen forward over one eye. It made her seem as though she was hiding from the bad news he was bringing.

He spoke softly. 'In short, it's an old picture but not a very good one. I can't put an exact figure on it but it's worth hundreds at the most, not thousands. Sorry.'

He placed his cigar back in his mouth. People, he had found, responded to the bad news in one of three ways. There were those who let their disappointment show. There were those who laughed it off—nervously; they were disappointed too. And there were those who had never really believed in the first place that they could be lucky enough to have stumbled across something truly valuable. They sometimes let their resentment turn into anger and would storm out of the gallery.

Isobel Sadler did none of these things. One eyebrow rose a fraction. She tapped her teeth with a fingernail, pushed her hair back from her eye and said, 'Yes, you've confirmed what I thought.'

Though Michael was genuinely passionate about

cigars, and smoked them in the bath or when he was fishing, there were occasions in the art business when they were useful to hide behind, to buy time. He could puff regularly, without speaking. It was almost as if cigar smoke contained some sort of soporific. People accepted delay more willingly. He played for time.

Isobel Sadler was an odd lady, he reflected. As odd as her picture. Before he could say anything, however, Patrick appeared with the coffee. The young man set the tray on a side-table and handed the cups across. Michael waited for him to leave before saying, 'If you knew the picture was nothing special, why bother to come? It was a waste of time after all—'

'I didn't say that!' Isobel Sadler didn't exactly shout but there was something—an edge—in her tone and Michael was brought up short. His coffee cup rattled in its saucer.

She went on, the edge still there in her voice. 'I agree that on the face of it this picture has little or no value, Mr Whiting. I have a soft spot for it—mainly because it's been in my family forever. But that doesn't blind me to the fact that it is not—well, a fine work. I come from an old West Country family and there is a tradition that Holbein was a friend of our ancestors. But I never really believed this was by him. As you say, a lot of it is clumsy and the composition is—well, you called it odd and I wouldn't disagree. If I didn't have a soft spot for it I would probably think it horrible.' She looked at Michael fiercely, as if to say that he didn't need to be gentle in his professional opinions with *her*.

'But—and this is the odd thing—I *do* think it may be special. Now I can get to the mystery. It's not how valuable this picture is, or who painted it, but why, two nights ago, someone tried to steal it.'

Michael set down his coffee cup. The sharp way in which Isobel Sadler had addressed him had caused him to flush slightly. He did not reply for a moment but sat, coaxing the smoke out of his cigar. His sister had a sharp tongue: Robyn would like the woman opposite. Then he said, 'That proves nothing. Thieves don't always know about art. They could have tried to take it by mistake or, because it was "art", imagined that it must be valuable.'

'No,' she said quickly. 'The thief made straight for the painting. I know because he woke me up breaking in and I disturbed him. I don't have any Ming in the house, or silver. But there's the usual hi-fi equipment. Thieves always go for electronic stuff first, or so I've been told. What's more, after I interrupted him—I managed to hit him in the shin with a vase that I threw at him—he escaped on a motorcycle. He could never have carried bulky hi-fi equipment on that. No, he definitely came for the painting.'

Michael pretended to examine the leaves of his cigar. The idea of this woman lobbing a vase at a burglar fascinated him. She was clearly a brave lady—but then the tone in her voice had told him she was red-blooded. Another thought struck him. If she was tackling burglars single-handed, did that mean she lived alone? He could feel her gaze fixed on him, the calculating eyebrows. 'You may be right, you may be wrong,' he said. 'I don't know. What I do know is that no amount of interest in this picture by thieves can make it valuable. It's not.'

Isobel Sadler's hair had fallen over her eye again and she brushed it away impatiently. 'I'm telling you my story backwards, Mr Whiting, and that is probably confusing. I apologise. I haven't told you about the coincidence yet. I wanted to be sure that it meant something. The fact that you confirm the picture is worthless only makes the coincidence more marked.'

Michael said nothing. A layer of lazy smoke drifted between them. As it approached Isobel Sadler she pointedly waved it away.

'I said I had a mystery for you, but the picture is only part of it. I suppose I should tell you something about myself—it will help. My family, the Sadlers, can trace our ancestors back to Tudor times. We are no longer rich'—she held up her hands—'I have had to work my parents' farm since they are both dead—but yes, we go back many generations.' Her eyes probed his. 'We have one famous ancestor—or perhaps "notorious" is a better word. Sir William Sadler: 1480 to 1537.' She smiled. 'I can never forget his dates. Anyway, he had a rather controversial role in the dissolution of the monasteries—he was called a "Visitor" and his job was to help Henry VIII dispose of all their assets, so it didn't exactly make him popular. The point is that because of Sir William—"Bad Bill" we called him in the family—I've always been interested in history, especially local history, anything to do with the family or the area we come from, near Painswick in Gloucestershire. For instance, I get all the catalogues of the manuscript sales at the auction houses, and a few weeks ago I noticed that some papers relating to Bad Bill were due to come up for auction at Sotheby's.'

She rubbed an eyebrow with her knuckle. 'For most people I would imagine they are thoroughly boring. They consisted of inventories mainly, relating to monasteries which Sir William had had a hand in dissolving, and there were a few letters he'd written, including one to another member of the family. That's what I was mainly interested in. They weren't expensive—a hundred and fifty to three hundred and fifty pounds for the lot. I thought I would have no bother getting them.' She smiled.

'But you did?' Michael had no idea why he was listening to this story, which had nothing to do with art.

Isobel Sadler nodded. 'I started bidding at the low end of the estimate: one hundred and fifty pounds. But there was someone else just as interested as me. I got carried away and so did this other person. The price went over five hundred pounds. Then to six hundred. I was astonished. At seven hundred pounds I had to drop out—the farm is a real drain just now.'

For a moment it was as if Isobel Sadler had left the room, so preoccupied was her expression, and Michael suspected that the farm was rather more than a drain. He glanced again at her rough hands. This woman was obviously having to work as a farm labourer herself.

But then, just as suddenly as she had left, she returned. 'I sat for a few moments after the lot had been knocked down. I was sort of stunned, I suppose. I didn't know who had beaten me but it didn't matter. I know that sometimes, at big sales, the underbidder will offer the winner a quick profit after the auction proper has ended, but I was so far over my limit anyway that, in my case, it was out of the question. There was no possibility I could offer any more. I started to leave—and that's when a man came up to me.'

Michael leaned forward. 'Your rival?'

Again she nodded. 'I learned later that his name was Molyneux. As I got up and struggled to the end of the row he helped me out. I thanked him and he said he'd seen me bidding and asked if I was a dealer. I said no. Then I explained my interest in the documents, just as I've explained to you. He apologised, saying he'd bought them on commission for someone else, an American. He walked out with me, making small talk, asking me where I lived, what else I collected and so on. He was very tall and towered over me. He towered over everyone. There were creases in his cheeks, I remember that. Outside on the pavement, he said he or his partner might be down in Gloucestershire in a few days and could he call? That's when he gave me his name. He also promised to ask the man on whose behalf he'd bought the documents whether he could send me some photocopies. It would be better than nothing, he said, and he might be able to drop them off if he stopped by.

'Then I forgot all about it. I never imagined he would call—it was just small talk. But he did. He didn't phone in advance, just turned up late one morning. He said he'd been visiting a house sale near Cirencester and had taken time off to visit me. I was half impressed and half puzzled. He had no news on the documents; he said his client was abroad and he had to wait for him to return before he could do anything. But he was hopeful, he said. I gave him some coffee, we chatted and he asked if he could look round the house. I gave him a very quick tour since I had to get back to the farm.'

'You showed him the picture?'

She nodded. 'He actually laughed when he first saw it, pointing out how odd it was, just as you did a few minutes ago. He asked how long I'd had it. I told him it had been in the family forever—I inherited it from my father, he from his father and so on. Anyway, after Molyneux had examined the painting we went on round the rest of the house and he began to talk about the curiosities he himself collected. He said he was reviving the old tradition of the fifteenth and sixteenth centuries, when people like the Hapsburgs had curio chambers with things like stuffed dodos, pictures of bearded ladies or notorious murderers, perpetual-motion machines or gems that were supposed to have magical properties. He said he would love to have the picture for his collection and offered me a thousand pounds for it. He suggested I might use the money to make an offer to the man who had bought the "Bad Bill" documents. In effect I would be swapping the picture for the papers.' She brushed her hair away from her eye again. 'I nearly said yes. But then I thought: if the man didn't agree to sell the documents to me I would have lost both them and the painting. So in the end I said no. Molyneux was charming. He said he quite understood, and left soon after. Then came the coincidence. Three days after his visit someone tried to steal the same picture.'

She drank some coffee, which by now must have been completely cold. Swallowing, she closed her eyes and bunched her eyebrows together. 'Too strong,' she gasped. 'Tell your boy not to brew it for so long.' Nonetheless, she drank again. The talk and the cigar smoke had no doubt made her throat dry. She waved the cigar smoke away again. Swallowing a second time, she went on. 'The more I thought about it, the more Molyneux's visit seemed odd. I even checked with all the estate agents in Cirencester—there aren't that many.' She placed her cup and saucer back on the tray. 'There hasn't been a house sale there for months.'

Michael went to interrupt but she waved him down.

'I think this man Molyneux came down to my house for a snoop. He was prepared to lie about the house sale, he was prepared to offer a thousand pounds for this picture, though you say it's probably not worth it, and now someone has been prepared to break into my house to steal the very same thing. I'll tell you something else. Molyneux is very tall, six feet four maybe. So was the burglar.' She looked intently at Michael. 'There's something about this picture, some mystery, that makes it worth stealing. It may have something to do with the documents I failed to buy and it may not. Anyway, Edward Ryan, who was a friend of my father when he collected Far Eastern art, said it was a mystery just up your street. I don't know where it will lead or if there's any money in it—but I'm willing to go halves with you on whatever you turn up. Edward said that would appeal to your gambling instincts.' She rubbed an eyebrow with her knuckle again. 'Does it?'

Michael rolled the Havana between his fingers. He blew out some smoke, but directed it away from Isobel Sadler. He tried the coffee—yes, it was cold. He turned over in his mind what she had told him. For openers it was a crazy story. More, he rather thought that Ryan and Isobel Sadler were overrating his ability to search out a particular mystery—he had never encountered anything like this before.

She held her hand to her throat. The smooth skin of her neck contrasted strongly with the roughness of her hands—yes, she needed money all right. The farm must be a fight but...the picture just wasn't good enough to pursue.

At length he said, 'I admit it was a coincidence about this man Molyneux's visit and the burglary, but coincidences happen all the time. That's often all they are: coincidences.'

'Why should he lie about the house sale in Cirencester?'

'People lie all the time, often for no very good reason.'

'All right, then, I'll give you another reason to help me. I've lived alone for a year and a half now, since my father died. I'm hanging on to the farm, but only just. I've got a manager but that's all. I can't afford to hire any more labour, so I have to work the land myself. I've been scared since the break-in, though I never was before. I simply can't afford an expensive alarm system. So I'd like to get the damn picture away from the house, even if it isn't worth anything. On the other hand, if it is, even a few thousands, it would come in very handy.'

'But it *isn't* worth anything,' Michael said. 'I'm certain of it.'

'Bah! Don't you dealers ever make mistakes?' She coughed and batted a cloud of cigar smoke away from her. 'I seem to read about them from time to time in the newspapers. Isn't there *any* research you can do? Maybe Holbein painted a bit of it, or perhaps it once belonged to somebody famous. That would add to its value, wouldn't it? Please don't say no.' She suddenly looked much less composed than before. Her hair had fallen forward again and this time she let it just hang there. 'I don't want to give up the picture, but I don't want it at home just now, either. *Please!*'

Was she acting? She didn't look the type to scare easily but being alone in a big farmhouse was, Michael supposed, very different from living in his own small house in the middle of Chelsea. He saw that her cheeks had flushed. They had a pink bloom like the woman's face in the painting which old Julius was restoring. That helped to make up his mind. The woman in Dover Street might well be an unsought-for bonus. If so, he could probably afford to spend some time on this other woman in front of him, even though Greg wouldn't thank him for taking on the extra burden.

'All right, all right. You walk in here out of the blue, you insult me, you criticise the coffee and make rude gestures about my cigars. Irresistible. Enbloodychanting.' But then he smiled and nodded. 'I'll take it off your hands—but at a price, and only for a week or so. If I can't find out anything in that time I'll have to hand it back. Is that a deal?'

'What do you mean, "at a price"?'

'Edward Ryan was not quite right. I'm not so much a gambling man as one who likes a wager. The difference matters, at least to me and my friends. I don't bet on the horses or play cards and I can't stand roulette, not for long anyway. That phone call you overheard just now was me practising my vice. Apart from this cigar, of course. And my whisky drinking and my chocolate habit.' He smiled. 'You won't have heard yet since we've been cooped up in here but it has just been announced that the film actress, Margaret Masson, has been divorced for the fifth time. Now, I belong to a small wagering club. Very small, only six members. Every January the first we each put up two thousand pounds, the money going to the one who, by the following Christmas, thinks up the most amusing wager. We don't do it regularly, only when something in the news crops up that takes our fancy. The stakes for the wagers are limited to a hundred pounds each, but at the end of the year we vote on who has had the best idea in the previous twelve months. The lucky man pockets ten thousand pounds—a nice Christmas present. That was a friend on the phone, a member of the club. His idea—and it's a good one—is that we wager on how long it is before Miss Masson announces her next engagement. You heard me opt for three weeks.'

'What you do in your spare time is your own business—but why are you telling me this?'

'Because I'm going to propose a wager to you.'

'I don't gamble.'

'Don't be such a prig. And I haven't told you the wager yet.'

Isobel Sadler said nothing.

'Don't worry, I have only mild vices.' He noticed that his cigar was going out and put a match to it. He rolled the leaves in the flame and flooded the room with billows of smoke. 'Dinner.'

She looked at him.

'If I find out *anything* about your picture that you didn't know and which increases its value, you agree to have dinner with me one of the times you are in London.'

'Do you often have dinner with strange women?'

'You're not that strange. Rita Hayworth wouldn't have worn that kilt, and you seem to like cold coffee, but no other oddities, as far as I can see.'

She smiled. 'I don't know whether I want to win or lose this bet—I mean wager.'

'Then you accept?'

'On condition that you don't smoke one of those filthy objects until the very end.'

'Done.'

'Thank you,' she breathed, quickly getting to her feet.

'I was beginning to think the picture was bringing me bad luck.' She began fiddling with her belt. 'I come up to London one evening a week—I have to get away from the farm one night or I'd go crazy. Shall I look in next week?'

'No.' He put the coffee cups back on the tray. 'Give me a fortnight. There are other things I have to do, you know,' he said, smiling. 'I have a gallery to run, cigars to buy, wagers to win.' They shook hands.

'Very well. Two weeks it is. Expect me at the same time as today.'

He opened the door and showed her through to the main gallery. Michael pointed to a watercolour of some stone houses. 'That was painted not far from you, in Broadway, Worcestershire. It's a Sargent. He lived there for a while. Henry James used to visit him.'

They both looked at the picture, then Michael opened the gallery door. Isobel Sadler hesitated at the main entrance into Mason's Yard and said, 'It's a beautiful gallery, Mr Whiting.'

'Thank you.'

'Yes. How would I describe it?' She paused, an eyebrow raised in the sharpest angle he'd yet seen. '"Well worth a detour"?'

Don't miss
The Godwin Sideboard,
another "Tim Simpson" art-mystery
by John Malcolm
coming in 2008 from
Felony & Mayhem Press